Edmund Hodgson Yates

The Rock Ahead

A novel. Vol. 2

Edmund Hodgson Yates

The Rock Ahead
A novel. Vol. 2

ISBN/EAN: 9783337213695

Printed in Europe, USA, Canada, Australia, Japan

Cover: Foto ©Andreas Hilbeck / pixelio.de

More available books at **www.hansebooks.com**

THE ROCK AHEAD.

LONDON :

ROBSON AND SON, GREAT NORTHERN PRINTING WORKS,

PANCRAS ROAD, N.W.

THE ROCK AHEAD.

A Novel.

BY

EDMUND YATES,

AUTHOR OF

'BLACK SHEEP,' 'KISSING THE ROD,' 'THE FORLORN HOPE,' ETC.

'The Gods are just ; and of our pleasant vices
Make instruments to scourge us.'

IN THREE VOLUMES.

VOL. II.

LONDON:

TINSLEY BROTHERS, 18 CATHERINE ST. STRAND.

1868.

CONTENTS OF VOL. II.

THE ROCK AHEAD.

CHAPTER VIII.

THE LINNET'S FIRST FLIGHT.

THERE were many phases of this life in which Lord Sandilands enjoyed a singular and an extensive popularity, many varieties of the social scale in which his name was mentioned with respect, and not a few in which he was regarded with far more than ordinary interest. In the first place, he was a man well born and well bred, and did honour to his position by his appearance, his manners, and the constant decorum which pervaded and formed part of his life. City merchants, members of parliament, who, having swept out their own counting-houses, of course became rigidest Conservatives, when by those wonderful gradations which are known to the reverent as "honest perseverance," and to the irreverent as "lucky flukes," they rose to be heads of the firm, felt immensely honoured by being permitted to play in the same rubber at the Portland with the calm, quiet, self-possessed, bald-headed, silver-fringed old nobleman, who was a model of courtesy throughout the game, but who never missed a point or gave a chance. Young men imbued with slang, as are the young men of the present day, dropped the metaphor of the prize-ring, music-hall, and the *demi-monde* villa in the presence of the "high-dried old boy," of whose position there could not be the smallest doubt, and who, on occasion, had shown that he owned a tongue which could make itself felt "doosid unpleasantly, don't you know!—kind of rough side of it, and all that sort of thing, you know!" To women he was always scrupulously attentive, and was in consequence in the greatest favour amongst them. The fact of his wearing the willow for his old love, Lady Lucy Beecher, was *répandu* from Belgrave- to Grosvenor-squares; and the

story, which had won for him such affectionate
interest amongst those who were young at the
time when, as all supposed, he was jilted by the
fair one, and bore his jilting so manfully, yet
lived amongst their descendants, and caused Lord
Sandilands to be regarded as " a sweet old thing,"
who had suffered in Love's cause, by *débutantes*
who were unborn when John Borlase first won
Gertrude Gautier's childish heart.

And yet Lord Sandilands was by no means
a representative man. For politics he cared little
or nothing. On special occasions he went down
to the House and voted with his party, but in
that was comprised his whole Parliamentary career. He never spoke and never intrigued: the
Custom-house and the Inland Revenue enrolled no
members who had obtained their appointments
at his instance; his personal appearance was unknown to the private secretary of the Postmaster-
general; nor was his handwriting to be found in
the bulging pigeon-holes of the Treasury. Man
years had elapsed since he had arrayed himself
in the charming court-costume which intelligence

has retained from the customs of the dark ages, and presented himself at the levees of his sovereign. At flower-shows and races, at afternoon Park or morning Row, at garden-parties or *fêtes champêtres*, at none of those gatherings where pleasant Frivolity rules, was Lord Sandilands known—at none, rather, save one—the Opera. There he was *facile princeps;* there he was king of the place. The check-takers and the box-keepers knew him as well as they knew the lessee, and stood in as much awe of him. The principal librarians, Messrs. Ivory, MacBone, and Déloge, prostrated themselves before him, and were always most anxious to learn his opinion of any novelty, as on that opinion they were accustomed to base their calculation of profit or loss. With Schrink, the critic of the *Statesman*—a cynical, hump-backed man, who had a spite against mankind, and "took it out" in writing venomous articles abusive of the world in general, and the musical world in particular—Lord Sandilands was the only man who had the smallest weight; and many a neophyte has owed the touch of oil which she received, instead of the pickling which threatened her, to a kind word dropped by his lordship in the seclusion of that box on the pit tier to which he alone was admitted, where Schrink sat nursing his leg, biting his nails, and glowering with fury alike at singers and audience. Behind the scenes his popularity was equally great; the sulky tenors gave up sucking their cough-lozenges and grinding their teeth at his approach, and welcomed him with courteous salutations; the basso roused himself from his stertorous sleep; the prima donna gave up that shrill altercation with her snuffy old mother; the property-men and the scene-shifters, who dashed indiscriminately against the gilded youth who roamed vacantly about, took special care to steer clear of Lord Sandilands, and touched their paper caps to him as he passed by; and the little ballet-women and chorus-singers dropped deepest curtsies to his lordship, and felt that so long as he was 'satisfied with them their pound a week was safe.

Had he any interest in the management? That was a moot point. Ever since the publi-

cation of the bankrupt's schedule made patent
the fact that a well-known advertising teacher of
languages was identical with an even more noto-
rious agricultural-implement maker, one has been
afraid to give any positive opinion as to who is
who in this most extraordinary world of ours.
Mr. Boulderson Munns was the responsible lessee
of the Grand Opera, and held the reins of management; but whose was the money embarked in
the speculation it was impossible to say. Young
Jeffcock, the China merchant (Jeffcock Brothers
of Shanghai), used to attend all the rehearsals,
had boxes always at his command, and was treated
with great deference by Mr. Boulderson Munns;
but in all these respects he was equalled by Jack
Clayton of the Coldstreams, who was notoriously
impecunious, who owed even for his button-hole
bouquets, and who spent all his ready-money in
hansom cabs and sprat-suppers for the *corps de
ballet*. Tommy Toshington, who knew most
things, declared that Lord Sandilands had no
monetary interest in the house, but that his position gave him greater influence with Mr. Boulder-

son Munns than was enjoyed by any of the others.
"Sandilands, sir," Tommy would say, when he
had dined well at somebody else's expense, —
"Sandilands is the man to give a stamp to a thing
of that sort! Don't know what there is in him,
but there's something that when he says a musical
thing's all right, it's safe to go. Why, when that
old gray horse and green brougham of his are seen
at the door of Canzonet's shop, as they are day
after day in the season, it's worth a fortune to
Sam Canzonet—he told me so himself. Money?
Not a sixpence, not a sous. When he was John
Borlase he was a regular screw, and he's not improved with age; but it is not money Munns
wants out of him. Jeffcock? nonsense! Jack
Clayton? bah! The real capitalist there, sir, is
—;" and here Mr. Toshington whispered in your
ear the name of a well-known Evangelical M.P.,
whom you would have as soon accredited with
Mormonism as with connection with theatrical
affairs; and having made his point, hobbles off
chuckling.

There was truth in this, although it was said

by Tommy Toshington. There was no doubt
that Lord Sandilands had powerful interest in
all the ramifications of the musical world; and
though this fact must for a long time have been
patent to him, he never thought of it, never, at
least, felt it so strongly as when he was turning
over in his mind the curious chance which had
brought him face to face with his daughter, and
had been casting about as to how he best could
serve her. That the girl had musical talent he
was certain. He had served too long an appren-
ticeship, all amateur though it was, to his favourite
science not to be thoroughly convinced of that;
and he knew perfectly well that Grace Lambert's
voice and style were both far beyond those possessed by most of the gifted pupils of the Academy
of Music: for the most part delightful young persons, who came out with a gush, and went in with
a run; who gave immense delight to their personal friends at the few concerts at which they
sung gratuitously; and who may, according to
the orthodox ending of the children's tales, "have
lived happy ever after," but who, at all events,

passed the remainder of their lives in obscurity,
and were never heard of again.

No; Grace Lambert—what the deuce had
made her assume so unromantic a name? Gertrude Keith was fifty times as pretty—Grace
Lambert was not to be measured by the usual
bushel. Her voice, as Lord Sandilands recollected it at Carabas House, was one of the
sweetest, the most *trainante* and bewitching
which, in all his great experience, he had ever
listened to; and there was something about her
personal appearance, her hair and *tournure*, which
completely lifted her out of the common. "Psht!"
said the old gentleman to himself, as he lay back
in his easy-chair, revolving all these things in his
mind—"how many of 'em have I seen? There
was Miss Lavrock—charmin' voice she had, bright
and shrill, like a bird's pipe—a little fat, dumpy
body, that made the plank in the *Sonnambula*
creak beneath the weight of her ten stone, and
looked more like a cook than Lucia; and there
was Miss Greenwood—Miss Bellenden Greenwood, I beg her pardon—with her saucy black

eyes, and her red-and-white complexion, and her corkscrew ringlets—gad, how horrible! But this child is marvellously *distinguée* and bred-looking; the way her head is set on her shoulders, the shape of her head, the curve of her nostrils, and the delicacy of her hands—I'm always telling myself that blood's all bosh, as they say in their modern slang; but 'pon my word, one finds there's something in it after all!"

Lord Sandilands was a constant visitor now at the pretty Bayswater villa, and had conducted himself with such courtesy and kindness as to render his presence anything but disagreeable to Grace. The time during which she had lived with her husband, short though it had been, had been quite long enough to give her an unconquerable aversion for slanginess and bad taste, and enable her to appreciate the spirit of the gentleman, which showed itself in every action, in every word of the old nobleman. Nor did Lord Sandilands, after a little time, care to conceal the great interest which he took in Miss Lambert's career. While carefully veiling everything which might show the relationship in which he stood to the young girl, and while never ceasing to impress on Mrs. Bloxam—much to that worthy woman's secret annoyance, for was she not the possessor of a secret even more mysterious and more compromising in connection with Gertrude?—the necessity of reticence, Lord Sandilands confessed to Miss Lambert that, actuated by the purest and most honourable motives, he wished to place himself at her service in advancing her interests in the profession which she had chosen, and in which she was evidently destined to take a high position, and in being of use to her in society. And in both these ways the old nobleman was of the greatest assistance to the *débutante*. As has been before said, his verdict in musical matters was immensely thought of; while, though it must be acknowledged that the open and avowed support of many elderly noblemen would be anything but fortunate in securing the interests of a young musical lady with the members of her own sex, that of such a known Galahad as Lord Sandilands had due weight, and his *protégée*, duly escorted by Mrs.

Bloxam, " went everywhere." " Everywhere" in-
cluded Lady Lowndes'; and the Marchioness of
Carabas knew of this, as how could she do otherwise? being a diligent student of the *Morning
Post,* in addition to having it told her by seven
of her dearest and most intimate friends, who
called for the express purpose of startling her with
the information during the next afternoon. But
the Marchioness knew of Miss Lambert's appearance at Lady Lowndes' house, and yet received
her the next day with a welcome which had in it
even more than the usual *empressement.* Why?
impossible to say, save that people were beginning
to talk more and more of Miss Grace Lambert's
voice and appearance, and specially of her manners. " Something odd about her, don't you know?
—frigid, unimpressionable, something-which-one-
can't-make-out sort of thing, you know!" the
ladies said; while the delightful creature in the
Blues, to whom she had been specially introduced with the view of eliciting the speaking of
her heart, declared she was " doosid hard nut to
crack," and something which had beaten him, the

delightful creature in the Blues, "by chalks."
So that Lady Carabas, carefully noting all the
phases of society, felt more bound than ever to
"keep in" with the *protégée* whom she had introduced; and the ambrosial footmen with the
powdered locks went more frequently than ever
between the halls of Carabas and the Bayswater
villa, and the much-monogramed notes which
they conveyed were warmer than ever in their
expressions of admiration and attachment, and
hopes of speedily seeing their most charming
&c.; and more than ever was Lady Carabas
Miss Grace Lambert's dearest friend. But Lady
Carabas was a very woman after all, and as such
her friendship for her dearest friend stopped at a
certain point; she brooked no interference in matters where her Soul (with the big S) was concerned. Other women, not possessing so much
worldly knowledge, might have given their dearest
friends opportunity for intimacy with the temporary possessor of the Soul, and then quarrelled
with them for causing the Soul to be depressed
with the pangs of jealousy and distrust. Lady

Carabas knew better than that. He whose image
the Soul, however temporarily, enshrined must be
kept sacred and apart, so far as it was possible to
keep him, and must be troubled with no tempta-
tion. Hence it happened that Gilbert Lloyd,
then regnant over Lady Carabas' Soul, was never
permitted to meet, or scarcely even to hear of,
the young lady in whom he would have recognised
his wife.

Of Miles Challoner, however, Miss Grace Lambert saw a great deal; not, indeed, at Carabas
House. Ever since the eventful evening of his
introduction to Mr. Gilbert Lloyd, Miles had
crossed the threshold of Lady Carabas' mansion
as seldom as social decency, in deference to the
Marchioness's constantly renewed invitations,
would permit him. The invitations were constantly renewed; for Lady Carabas had taken
a liking to the young man, and, indeed, the idea
had crossed her ladyship's mind that when Gilbert
Lloyd's time of office had expired—and his tenure
had been already more than the average—she
could scarcely do better than intrust Miles Chal-

loner with the secret of the existence of her Soul, and permit him to share in its aspiration. There was a freshness, she thought, about him which would suit her admirably; a something so different from those *fades* and jaded worldlings among whom her life was passed. But though the invitations were constant, the response to them was very limited indeed, and only on one or two occasions subsequent to his introduction did Miles avail himself of the hospitality of Carabas House. On none of these occasions did he meet Mr. Gilbert Lloyd. The same reason which induced Lady Carabas to manœuvre in keeping her friend for the time being from meeting her handsome *protégée* suggested to her the expediency of preventing any possible collision between the actual and the intended sharers of her Soul; collision, as Lady Carabas thought, by no means unlikely to occur, as she was a shrewd observant woman of the world, and had noticed the odd behaviour of both gentlemen at the time of their introduction.

But Lord Sandilands, loving Miles Challoner

for his own and for his father's sake, and noticing
the strong impression which Miss Lambert's voice
and beauty had made upon the young man, had
taken him to the Bayswater villa, and formally
introduced him; and both Mrs. Bloxam and Grace
had "hoped they should see more of him." He
was a gentleman. You could not say much more
of him than that; but what an immense amount
is implied in that word! He was not very bright;
he never said clever or smart things—consequently
he kept himself from evil-speaking, lying, and
slandering; he had no facility for gossip—consequently he never intruded on the ladies the latest
news of the *demi-monde* heroines, nor the back-
stairs' sweepings of the Court; he was earnest and
manly, and full of youthful fervour on various
subjects, which he discussed in a bright, modest
way which won Mrs. Bloxam's by no means impulsive heart, and at the same time made that
impulsive heart beat quickly with its knowledge
of Gertrude's secret: a secret with which the
unexpressed but impossible-to-be-mistaken admiration of this young man might interfere.

Impossible-to-be-mistaken admiration? Quite impossible. Lord Sandilands—though years had gone by since he had been a proficient in that peculiar vocabulary, whose expressions are undefined and untranslatable—recognised it in an instant, and scarcely knew whether to be pleased or vexed as the idea flashed upon him. He loved Miles like his own son, believed in all his good qualities, recognised and admitted that the young man had all in him requisite to make a good, loving husband; his social status, too, was such as would be most desirable for a girl in Gertrude's position. But Lord Sandilands knew that any question of his natural daughter's marriage would entail the disclosure of the relation in which he stood to her; and he dreaded the ridicule of the world, dreaded the banter of the club, dreaded more than all the elucidation of the fact that the *répandu* notion of his wearing the willow for Lady Lucy Beecher had been all nonsense, and that he had consoled himself for her ladyship's defalcation by an intrigue of a very different calibre.

"I should be laughed at all over town,"
the old gentleman said to himself; "and though
it must come, by George, it's best to put off
the evil day as long as possible. I don't know.
I'm an old fellow now, and have not as keen an
eye for these things as I had; but *I* don't perceive any sign of a *tendresse* on Gertrude's part;
and, all things considered, I'm glad of it."

And Lord Sandilands was right. There was
not the smallest sign of any feeling for Miles
Challoner in Grace Lambert. Had she had the
least spark of such a feeling kindling in her heart,
it is very doubtful whether she would have permitted it to be remarked in her outward manner;
but her heart was thoroughly free from any such
sentiment. She liked Miles Challoner—liked his
frank bearing, and was touched, after her fashion,
by the respect which he showed her. It was
something quite new to her, this old-fashioned
courtesy from this young man. Of course, during
her schooldays she had seen nothing of mankind,
save as exemplified in the foreign professors of
languages and music, whose courtesy was for the

most part of the organ-monkey order—full of
bows and grins. After her marriage, the set in
which she was thrown—though to a certain extent kept in order by the feeling that Gilbert
Lloyd was "a swell," and had peculiar notions
as to how his wife should be treated—never had
scrupled to talk to her without removing their
hats, or to smoke in her presence. And though
the gentlemen she had met at Carabas House
had been guilty of neither of these solecisms,
there had been a certain *laissez-aller* air about
them, which Grace Lambert had ascribed to a
tant soit peu disdain of her artistic position; the
real fact being that to assume a vice if he have
it not, and to heap as much mud as possible on
that state of life into which it has pleased Provi-
dence to call him, is the chosen and favourite
occupation of a high-born and wealthy young
man of the present day. So Grace Lambert
recognised Miles Challoner as a gentleman *pur
sang*, and appreciated him accordingly; had a
bright glance and a kindly word of welcome for
him when he appeared at the Bayswater villa,

made him at home by continuing her singing-
practice while he remained, made him happy by
asking him when he was coming again as he said
his adieux; but as to having what Lord Sandilands called a *tendresse* for the man, as to being
in love with him — Love came into Gertrude
Keith's heart three months before she walked
out of the laundry-window over the roof of the
schoolroom, and stepped down on to the driving-
seat of the hansom cab, in which Gilbert Lloyd
was waiting to take her off to the church and
make her his wife. Love died out of Gertrude
Lloyd's heart within three months of that mar-
riage-day; and as for Grace Lambert, she never
had known and never intended to know what the
sentiment meant. So, so far, Lord Sandilands
was right; and the more he watched the conduct of the two young people when alone towards
each other—and he watched it narrowly enough
—the more he took occasion to congratulate
himself on his own perspicacity and knowledge
of the world. But at the same time he reflected
that the life which Miss Grace Lambert was

leading was but a dull one, that she took but little
interest in these society successes; and he took
occasion to glean from her what he knew before
—that her heart and soul were bound up in her
profession, and that she was by no means satisfied by the hitherto limited opportunities afforded
her of showing what she really could do therein.
This ambition of the girl's to make for herself
name and fame in the musical world by no means
jarred against the ideas of the old nobleman.
He should have to acknowledge her as his daughter some day or other, that he saw clearly
enough; and it would be infinitely preferable to
him, and would render him infinitely less ridiculous in the eyes of that infernal bantering club-
world of which he stood so much in awe, if he
could point to a distinguished artist of whom
all the world was talking in praise, and say,
"This is my child," than if he had to bear the
brunt of the parentage of a commonplace and
unknown person. There were half-a-dozen other
ladies occupying a somewhat similar position to
Miss Lambert's in society, as queens of amateur

singing sets; and though she was acknowledged by all disinterested people to be far and away the best of them, it was necessary that she should have some public ratification of her merits, or, at all events, that some professional opinion, independent of that of Da Capo or her other singing-master, who would naturally be biassed, should be given. The other ladies were daughters and wives of rich men, who sang a little for their friends' and a great deal for their own amusement; but Miss Lambert's career was to be strictly professional, and a touchstone of a very different kind was to be applied to her merits.

That was a happy time for Miles Challoner, perhaps really the happiest in his life. His first love, at least the first passion really deserving that name, was nascent within him, and all the environing circumstances of his life were tinged with the roseate hue which is the necessary "local colour" of the situation. Moreover, his feelings towards Gertrude were at present in that early stage of love in which they could be borne and

indulged in without worrying and making him
miserable. She was the nicest woman he had
ever seen, and there was something marvellously
attractive about her, something which he could
not explain, but the magnetic influence of which
he knew it impossible to resist. So he abandoned
himself to the enjoyment of this pleasant feeling,
enjoying it doubly perhaps, because up to this
point it had been, and seemed to promise to con-
tinue to be, a mild and equable flame; not
scorching and withering everything round it, but
burning with a pleasant, steady heat. You see,
at present Mr. Challoner had not seen much, if
anything, of Miss Lambert alone; his admiration
sprung from observation of her under the most
commonplace circumstances, and his passion had
never been quickened and stung into fiercer action
by the thought of rivalry. True, that whenever
Miss Lambert went into society she was always
surrounded by a bragging crowd of representa-
tives of the gilded youth of the period, who did
their best to flatter and amuse her; attempts in
which, if her grave face and formal manner

might be accepted in evidence, they invariably
and signally failed. And at the Bayswater villa
he might be said to have her entirely to himself,
he being the only young man admitted there, with
the exception occasionally of some musical pro-
fessor, native or foreign; the delightful creature
in the Blues, and other delightful creatures who
had made Miss Lambert's acquaintance in society,
having tried to obtain the *entrée* in vain.

So Miles went on pleasantly in a happy dream,
which was very shortly to come to an end; for
Lord Sandilands, thinking it full time that some
definite steps should be taken in regard to Gertrude's professional future, arrived one morning
at the Bayswater villa, and was closeted with the
young lady for more than two hours. During
this interview, the old gentleman, without betraying his relationship with her, told Gertrude that,
far beyond anything else, he had her interests at
heart; that he had perceived her desire for professional distinction; and that, as he saw it was
impossible to combat it, he was ready then and
there to advance it to the best of his ability.

Only, as the training was somewhat different, it was necessary that she should make up her mind whether she would prosecute her career in the concert-room or on the operatic stage.

It was a pity Miles Challoner was not present to mark the brilliant flush which lit up Gertrude's usually pale cheeks, the fire which flashed in her eyes, and the proud curl of her small lips, as this proposition was made to her. For a few moments she hesitated, a thousand thoughts rushed through her mind—thoughts of her real position, retrospect of her past life—a wild, feverish vision of future triumph, where she, the put-aside and rejected of Gilbert Lloyd, the pupil-teacher of the suburban boarding-school, should be queen regnant, and have some of the greatest and highest in the kingdom for her slaves. As *prima donna* of the Opera, what position might she not assume, or where should her sway stop, if ambition were to be gratified? And then the old cynical spirit arose within her, and she thought of the tinsel and the sham, the gas and the gewgaws; and the light died out of her eyes, and her cheeks resumed their usual pallor, and it was a perfectly cold hand which she placed in Lord Sandilands', as she said to him, without the smallest tremor in her voice, " You have indeed proved yourself a perfectly disinterested friend, my lord ; how could I do better than leave the decision on my future career in your hands?"

Lord Sandilands was rather unprepared for this speech, and a little put out by it. He had an objection to accepting responsibility in general; and in this instance, where he really felt deeply, he thought naturally that Gertrude would scarcely think of him with much gratitude if his choice did not eventuate so happily for her as he intended. However, there was nothing else to be done; so he raised the cold hand to his lips with old-fashioned gallantry, and promised to " think the matter over," and see her again on the following day. With many people, to think a matter over means to discuss it with someone else. Lord Sandilands was of this class; and though he accepted the commission so glibly from Gertrude, he never had the smallest intention of deciding upon it without taking excellent advice. That advice he sought at the hands of Mr. Déloge, the "librarian" of Jasmin-street.

An odd man, Mr. Déloge—a character worth a passing study. His father, who had been a "librarian" before him, had amassed a large sum of money in those good old days when speculations in opera-boxes and stall-tickets were highly remunerative to those who knew how to work them, had given his son an excellent education abroad, and had hoped to see him take a superior position in life. But, to his parent's disappointment, young Déloge, returning from the Continent with a knowledge of several languages, and an acquaintance with life and the world which serves anyone possessing it better than any other knowledge whatsoever, determined to follow the family business, adding to it and grafting on to it such other operations as seemed to be analagous. These operations were so admirably selected and so well conducted, that before the old man died he had quite acquiesced in his son's decision, and

at the time of our story there was no more thriv-
ing man in London. The old-fashioned shop in
Jasmin-street bore the name over the door still ;
but that name was now widely known throughout England and Europe. No Secretary of State
was harder worked than Mr. Déloge, who yet
found time to hunt once or twice a week, to live
at Maidenhead during the summer, and at Brighton during the autumn, and generally to enjoy
life. In person he was a tall thin man, with an
excellently-made wig and iron-gray whiskers,
always calm and staid in demeanour, and always
irreproachably dressed after the quietest style.
He looked like a middle-aged nobleman whose
life had been passed in diplomacy; and people
who asked who he was—and most people did, so
striking was his appearance—were surprised to
hear that he was only "the man who sells the
stalls, don't you know?" in Jasmin-street. Nothing pleased him more than to observe this astonishment, and he used to delight in telling a
story against himself in illustration of it. One
day, in the course of business, he had occasion to

wait on a very great lady, one of his customers. He drove to the house in his perfectly-appointed brougham, and the door was opened by a strange footman, to whom he gave his card for transmission to her grace. The footman led the way into the library, poked the fire, wheeled the largest arm-chair in front of it, and placed the *Morning Post* in the visitor's hands. Mr. Déloge had scarcely finished smiling at the extreme *empressement* of the man's manner, when the door was opened, and the same servant pushed his head in. "Her grace don't want no hop'ra-box tonight," were his charming words, delivered in his most offensive manner. The scales had fallen from his eyes, and the great creature found he had deceived himself into being civil to a "person in business."

Mr. Déloge had gone through what to many men would have been an entire day's business in the morning before Lord Sandilands called upon him. He had read through an enormous mass of letters, and glanced over several newspapers—had pencilled hints for answers on some, and dictated replies to others at full length. His business seemed to have ramifications everywhere : in Australia, where he had an agent travelling with the celebrated Italian Opera *troupe*, the soprano, basso, tenor, and baritone, who were a little used up and bygone in England, but who were the greatest creatures that had ever visited Australia —so at least said the *Wong-Wong Kangaroo*, a copy of which the agent forwarded with his letter; in America, where Schlick's opera, in which Mr. Déloge possessed as much copyright as the large-souled American music-sellers could not pillage him of, was a great success; in India, whence he had that morning received a large order for pianos —for Mr. Déloge is not above the manufacture and exportation of musical instruments, and indeed realises a handsome yearly revenue from that source alone. Before eleven o'clock he had come to terms, and signed and sealed an agreement with Mr. McManus, the eminent tragedian, for a series of readings and recitations throughout the provinces, thus giving the " serious" people who objected to costume and gas a quasi-theatrical entertainment which they swallowed eagerly; he had sent a cheque for ten pounds to Tom Lillibullero, who was solacing his imprisonment in Whitecross-street by translating a French libretto for the house of Déloge; he had given one of his clerks a list of a few friends to be asked down to Maidenhead the next Sunday — all art people, writers, painters, singers, who would have a remarkably jolly day, and enjoy themselves, as they always do, more than any other set of people in the world; and he had written half-a-dozen private notes—one among the rest addressed to the Marchioness of Carabas, telling her that as her ladyship particularly wished it he should be happy to purchase and publish Mr. Ferdinand Wisk's operetta, which had been performed with such success at Carabas House, but that he must stipulate that the operetta must be dedicated to her ladyship, and that each *morceau* must have a vignette from her ladyship's portrait on the cover.

Mr. Déloge had not half completed his business for the day when he was informed, through the snake-like elastic pipe that lay at the right-hand of his writing-table, that Lord Sandilands was in the shop and asking to see him, but he gave orders that his visitor should at once be admitted. He was far too recognisant of the old nobleman's position in the musical world to have kept him waiting or allowed him to feel the smallest slight, if indeed there had not been, as there was, a feeling of respect between the two men, which, had they been on the same social footing, would have been strong friendship.

"How d'ye do, Déloge?" said Lord Sandilands, walking up and heartily shaking hands; "this is very kind of you, my good fellow, to allow me to come and bother you when you're over head and ears in business, as you always are—very kind indeed."

"I don't want to say a pretty thing, my dear lord," said Mr. Déloge, "but when I can't find leisure from my business to attend to you when you want to see me, I'd better give that business up."

"Thanks, very much. Well, what's the news?

Been to Tenterden - street lately? Any very promising talent making itself heard up there, eh?"

"No, my lord, none indeed—I'm glad to say," replied Déloge with a laugh.

"Glad to say! eh, Déloge? that's not very patriotic, is it?"

"O, I did not mean to confine my gladness to the dearth of native talent. If you only knew, my dear lord, how I'm hunted out of life by promising talent, or by talent which considers itself promising and wants to perform, you would know fully how to appreciate, as I do, good steady-going mediocrity."

"By Jove, Déloge! this is not very encouraging for me! I came to ask your advice on the question of bringing out a young lady of unquestionable genius."

"Unless her genius is quite unquestionable I should advise you to let the young lady remain in. Why, think for yourself, my dear lord; you know these things as well as I do, and have every singer for the past quarter of a century in your mind.

Run over the list and tell me which of them—
always excepting Miss Lavrock—has made anything like a success."

"Ha!" said Lord Sandilands, "yes, the Lavrock—what a voice, what a charming trill! not
but that I think Miss Lambert—"

"Is it a question of Miss Lambert — Miss
Grace Lambert?"

"It is. Miss Lambert has decided upon adopt-
ing the musical profession, and my object in coming here was to consult you as to the best means
to give effect to her wishes."

"That's quite another affair. I have only
heard Miss Lambert once. I was engaged by
Lady Lowndes to pilot Miramella and Jacowski
to one of her ladyship's wonderful gatherings, and
after they had finished their duet we went to the
dining-room to get some of that curious refresh-
ment which is always provided there for the artists. They had scarcely begun to eat when the
whole house rang with a trill of melody so clear
and bird-like that the Miramella only drank half
her glass of sherry, and Jacowski put down his

sandwich—I don't wonder at it—untasted. We all rushed upstairs, and found that the singer was Miss Grace Lambert. She sang so exquisitely, and produced such an immense effect, that Madame Miramella was seized with one of her violent headaches, and was obliged to be taken home."

Lord Sandilands was delighted. "Poor Miramella!" said he, chuckling quietly, "and Ger— and Miss Lambert was successful?"

"Successful! I have not heard such a combination of voice and style for years! But I thought she was merely an amateur, and had no idea she intended to take to the profession."

"Yes, she is determined to do so; and as I take the greatest interest in her, I have come to ask your advice. Now, should she select the concert-room or the stage as her arena?"

"The stage! the stage!" cried Déloge excitedly; "there can be no question about it, my dear lord! With that personal appearance and that voice, she must have the whole world at her feet, and make her fortune in a very few years. Any dumpy little woman who can sing tolerably

in tune, and face an audience without the music
in her hand visibly trembling, will do for a concert-room; but this young lady has qualities
which—Good heavens! fancy the effect she'd
make in Opera, with that head and that charming figure!"

"My good friend!" said the delighted old
nobleman, "you are becoming positively enthusiastic. In these days of total suppression of feelings, it does one good to hear you. I am charmed
to see you think so highly of my *protégée*. Now
tell me, what's the first step to be taken towards
bringing her out?"

"I should let Munns hear her," said Mr. Déloge.

And Lord Sandilands' face fell, and he looked
very grave. Why? Well, the mention of Mr.
Munns' name was the first thing that had jarred
disagreeably on Lord Sandilands' ears and feelings in connection with Gertrude's intended adop-
tion of the musical profession; and it *did* jar.
Why, Lord Sandilands knew perfectly, but could
scarcely express.

Who was Mr. Boulderson Munns? You might have asked the question in a dozen different sets of society, and received a different answer in each. What was his birth or parentage no one, even the veriest club scandal-monger, ever assumed to know; and as to his education, he had none. He had been so long " before the public" that people had forgotten whence he came, or in what capacity his *début* was made. Only a very few men remembered, or cared to remember, that when Peponelli's management of the Grand Scandinavian Opera came to smash disastrously, by reason of Miramella, Jacowski, Courtasson, and Herzogenbusch, the celebrated singers, revolting and going over in a body to the Regent Theatre, the opposition house, Messrs. Mossop and Isaacson, of Thavies' Inn, put themselves in communication with the agents of the Earl of Haremarch, the ground landlord, and proposed their client, Mr. Boulderson Munns, as tenant. Lord Haremarch's agent, old Mr. Finchingfield, of New-square, Lincoln's Inn, looked askance through his double eye-glass at Messrs. Mossop and Isaacson's letter. He had

heard of those gentlemen, truly, and knew them
to be in a very large way of business, connected
generally with people "in trouble"—criminals and
bankrupts. Of Mr. Boulderson Munns, the gentleman proposed as tenant, Mr. Finchingfield had
never heard ; but on consulting with Mr. Leader,
his articled clerk, a young gentleman who saw a
good deal of " life," he learned that Mr. Munns
had been for some time lessee of the Tivoli Gardens over the water, and was supposed to be a
shrewd, clever, not too scrupulous man, who knew
his business and attended to it. Mr. Finchingfield was a man of the world. " I don't know anything about such kind of speculations, and indeed
it is strongly against my advice that my Lord
Haremarch permits himself to be mixed up in
such matters," he said. " But I should imagine
that from a person tendering for a theatre you
do not require a certificate of character from the
clergyman of his parish ; and if Mr. Munns is
prepared to deposit a year's rent in advance, and
to enter into the requisite sureties for the due performance of the various covenants of the lease, I

see no reason why I should not recommend my
lord to accept him as his tenant." And Mr.
Leader, remembering this conversation, made a
point of letting Mr. Munns know as soon as possible that if he, Mr. Munns, should get the theatre
it would be owing entirely to his, Mr. Leader's,
representations,—a statement made by Mr. Leader
with a view to the future acquisition of gratuitous
private boxes, and that much coveted *entrée* known
as " going behind."

So Mr. Boulderson Munns became the tenant
of the Grand Scandinavian Opera House, and
took up his position in society, which at once
began to pick holes in his garments, and to say
all the unpleasant things it could against him.
Some people said his name was not Boulderson
at all, nor Munns much; that his real appella-
tion was Muntz, and that he was the son of a
German Jew sugar-baker in St. George's-in-the
East. People who professed to know said that
Mr. Munns commenced his career in the useful
though not-much-thought-of profession of a chiro-
podist, which they called a corn-cutter, in which

capacity he took in hand the feet of Polesco Il Diavolo, the gentleman who made a rushing descent down a rope with fireworks in his heels at the Tivoli Gardens; and that by these means the youthful Muntz was brought into relations with Waddle, who then owned the gardens, and to whom Muntz lent some of the money he had inherited from the parental sugar-baker, at enormous interest. When Waddle collapsed, Muntz first appeared as Munns, and undertook the management of the gardens, which he carried on for several years with great success to himself and gratification to the public—more especially to the members of the press, who were always free of the grounds, and many of whom were entertained at suppers, at which champagne — known to Mr. Munns by the name of "sham"—flowed freely. He was a genial, hospitable, vulgar dog, given, as are the members of his nation, to the wearing of rich-coloured velvet coats and waistcoats, and jewelry of a large and florid pattern, to the smoking of very big cigars, the driving of horses in highly-plated harness in mail-phaetons with

wheels vividly picked out with red, to the swearing of loud and full-flavoured oaths, and to Richmond dinners on the Sunday. When he entered
on the lesseeship of the Grand Scandinavian
Opera House, he continued all these eccentricities
of pleasure, but mixed with them some excellent
business habits. On the secession of Miramella,
Jacowski, and all the rest, the public pronounced
the Scandinavian Opera to be utterly dead and
done for; but after the first few weeks of his
season Mr. Munns produced Fraulein Brödchen,
from the Stockholm Theatre, who fairly routed
everyone else off their legs, and took London by
storm. Never had been known such a triumph
as that achieved by the Brödchen; boxes and
stalls fetched a fabulous price, and were taken
weeks in advance. It began to be perceived that
the right thing was that Norma should have
bright red hair; and people wondered how they
had for so long endured any representative of
Lucrezia without a turn-up nose. Miramella of
the classic profile and the raven locks was nowhere. Jacowski the organ-voiced bellowed in

vain. The swells of the Young-England party
—guardsmen and impecunious youths, who were
on the free list at the Regent—tried to get up an
opposition; but Munns ran over to Barcelona,
and came back with the Señorita Ciaja, whose
celebrated back-movement in the Cachuca finished
the business. The people who really understood
and cared for music were delighted with the Brödchen; the occupants of the stalls and the omnibus-
box—crabbed age and youth, who, despite the old
song, manage to live together sometimes, and on
each other a good deal—revelled in the Ciaja, and
the trick was done. Mr. Munns realised an enormous sum of money, and was spoken of everywhere as "a marvellous fellow! a cad, sir, but a
genius!"

He was a cad, there was no doubt of that.
The Earl of Haremarch, who, with all his
eccentricities, was a highly-polished gentleman,
suffered for days after an interview with his
tenant, who would receive him in his managerial room with open bottles of "sham," and
"My lord" him until the wine had done its

work, when he would call him "Haremarch, old
fellar!" with amiable frankness. He always addressed the foreign artistes in English; told them
he didn't understand their d—d palaver, and
poked them in the ribs, and slapped them on the
back, until they ground their teeth and stamped
their feet in inarticulate fury; but his money was
always ready when due, and his salaries were
liberal, as well as promptly paid. The *corps de
ballet* adored him, admired his velvet waistcoats,
and screamed at his full-flavoured jokes. In person, Mr. Munns was a short stout man, with an
enormous chest, a handsome Hebraic face, with
dyed beard and whiskers, and small keen eyes.

To such a man as this, Lord Sandilands, the
polished old nobleman, had naturally a strong an-
tipathy; and yet Lord Sandilands was almost the
only man of his *clientèle* to whom Mr. Munns
showed anything like real respect. "There's
something about that old buffer," he would say,
"which licks me;" and he could not have paid
a greater compliment. The Brödchen had retired into private life before this, and the Ciaja

had gone to America on a starring tour; but Mr.
Munns had replaced them with other attractions,
had well maintained his ground: and when Mr.
Déloge told Lord Sandilands that from Mr.
Munns it would be best to obtain the information and the opinion he sought, the old nobleman
knew that the librarian was right; though he
hated Mr. Munns from the bottom of his heart,
yet he made up his mind to get the great *impresario* to hear Miss Grace Lambert, and determined to abide by his advice.

So, one fine afternoon, the little road in which
the pretty Bayswater villa was situated was thrown
into a state of the greatest excitement by the arrival of the dashing phaeton with the prancing
horses in their plated harness; and Mr. Boulderson Munns alighting therefrom, was received by
Lord Sandilands, and duly presented to Miss
Lambert. After partaking somewhat freely—for
he was a convivial soul—of luncheon and dry
sherry—which wine he was pleased to compliment highly, asking the "figure" which it cost,
and the name of the vendor—the great *impresario*

was ushered into the drawing-room, where Signor Da Capo seated himself at the piano, and Gertrude, without the smallest affectation or hesitation, proceeded to sing. Mr. Munns, who had been present at many such inaugural attempts, seated himself near Lord Sandilands with a resigned countenance; but after a very few notes the aspect of his face entirely changed; he listened with the greatest attention; he beat time with his little podgy diamond-ringed fingers, and with his varnished boots; and at the conclusion of the song, after a strident cry of "Brava! brava!" he winked calmly at the radiant nobleman, laid his finger alongside his nose, and whispered, "Damme, that'll do!"

After a further hearing the great *impresario* expressed himself more fully, after his own symbolic fashion.

"That's the right thing," said he; "the right thing, and no flies! or rather it will be the right thing a few months hence.—My dear," he continued, laying his hand on Gertrude's arm, and keeping it there, though she shrank from his touch, "no offence, my dear; you've got the right stuff in you! No doubt of that! Now what we've got to do is to bring it out of you. Don't you make any mistake about it; it's there, but it wants forcing. What's to force it? why, a mellower air and a few lessons reg'larly given by someone who knows all about it. No offence again to Da Capo here, who's a very good fellow —him and me understand each other; but this young lady wants someone bigger than him, and quiet and rest and freedom from London ways and manners. Let her go to Italy and stop there for nine months; meanwhile you and me, my lord, the Marsh'ness Carabas, and the rest of us, will work the oracle, and then she shall come back and come out at the Grand Scandinavian Opera House; and if she ain't a success, I'll swallow my Lincoln and Bennett!"

There was a pause for a minute, and then Lord Sandilands said: "Do you mean that Miss Lambert should make her *début* on the Italian stage?"

"Not a bit of it," shrieked Mr. Munns; "keep her *début* for here! A gal like that, who

can walk up to the piano and sing away before
me, won't have any stage-fright, I'll pound it!
Let her go to Florence, to old Papadaggi—which
you know him well, my lord, and can make it
all square there; let her take lessons of him, and
make her *début* with me. I'm a man of my word,
as you know, and I see my way."

Within a fortnight from that time Miles Challoner, who had been out of town, called at the
Bayswater villa, found it in charge of a police-
man and his wife, learned that Miss Lambert
and Mrs. Bloxam had gone to Hit'ly for some
months, and—went away lamenting.

CHAPTER IX.

THE novelty of her life in Italy was full of charm for Gertrude. She was still so young that she could escape, in any momentary emotion of pleasure, from the hardening influence of the past, and the entire change of scene had almost an intoxicating effect upon her. Here was no association with anything in the past which could pain, or in the present which might have the power to disconcert her. Her husband's foot had never trodden the paths in which she wandered daily, with all the pleasure of a stranger and all the appreciation of natural beauty which formed a portion of her artistic temperament. He had never gazed upon the classic waters of the Arno, or roamed through the picture-galleries which afforded her such intense delight, and would have been almost without a charm for his

cynical materialistic nature. At least, if he had
ever visited Italy, Gertrude did not know it;
and with all her very real indifference, despite
the wonderfully thorough enfranchisement of her
mind and heart from the trammels of her dead-
and-gone relation to him, Gertrude, with true
womanly inconsistency, still occasionally associated him sufficiently with her present life to feel
that distance from Gilbert Lloyd, that the strangeness of the unfamiliar places with which he was
wholly unassociated, added to the reality of her
sense of freedom, gave it zest and flavour. She
understood this inconsistency. "If I go on like this,"
she would think, "it will never do. I am much
too near hating him at present to be comfortable.
So long as he is not absolutely nothing to me I
am not quite free; so long as I prefer the sense
of the impossibility of my seeing him by any
accident—so long as I am more glad to know
that he is staying with Lord Ticehurst, and Lord
Ticehurst's reputable friends, than I should be
to know that he was in the next house on the
promenade—so long as either circumstance has

the smallest appreciable interest or importance for me—I am not free. I must regard him as so utterly nothing, that if I were to meet him to-morrow at the Cascine, or passing my door, it could have no importance, no meaning for me. I don't mean only in the external sense, of not appearing to agitate or concern me, but in the interior convictions of my own inmost heart. Such freedom I am quite resolved to have. It will come, I am sure, but not just yet. I am far too near to hating him yet."

Gertrude had unusual power in the distribution of the subjects on which she chose to exercise her thinking faculty, and in the absolute and sustained expulsion from her mind of such topics as she chose to discard. This faculty was very useful to her now. There were certain phases and incidents of her life with Gilbert Lloyd which she never thought about. She deliberately put them out of her mind, and kept them out of it. Among these were the occurrences which had immediately preceded the strange bargain which had been made between

her and her husband. Of that bargain herself
she thought with ever-growing satisfaction, remembering with complacent content the obscurity
in which she had lived, which rendered such an
arrangement possible, without risk of detection.
But she never travelled farther back in memory
than the making of that bargain. So then she
determined to carry it out to the fullest, to have
all the satisfaction out of it she possibly could.
"I am determined I will bring myself to such
freedom that the sight of him could not give me
even an unpleasant sensation—that the sound of
his name announced in the room with me should
have no more meaning for me than any other
sound devoid of interest."

Gertrude was more happily circumstanced now
for the carrying out of this determination. All
her surroundings were delightful and novel, she
was in high health and spirits, and her prospects
for the future were bright and near. The climate
was enchanting, the hours and the ways of foreign
life suited her; and her masters pronounced her
voice all that could be desired in the case of a

daughter of sunny Italy, and something altogether admirable and extraordinary in the case of a daughter of foggy Albion. She worked very hard. She kept her ambition, her purpose steadily before her, and her efforts to obtain the power of gratifying it were unrelaxing.

Hitherto Gertrude's experiences had been those only of a school-girl and a woman married to an unscrupulous man who lived by his wits. She had never been out of England before; and the interval of her life at the villa, under the beneficial influence of the Carabas patronage, though very much pleasanter than anything she had before experienced, had not tended much to the enlargement and cultivation of her mind or the expansion of her feelings. But this foreign life did tend to both. She was entirely unfettered, and the sole obligation laid upon her was the vigilant precaution it was necessary she should observe against taking cold. It was in Gertrude's nature to prize highly this newly-acquired sense of personal freedom, and to enter with avidity into all that was strange in her life abroad. Her enjoyment of the difference between the habits and customs of Italy and those of England was unintelligible to Mrs. Bloxam, who had also never before been out of England, and who carried all the true British prejudice in favour of everything English with her. She could not be induced to admit the superiority of foreign parts even in those lesser and superfluous respects to which it is generally conceded. "I cannot see," she remarked to a sympathising soul, whose acquaintance she had made shortly after her arrival—a lady held in foreign bondage by a tyrannical brother and his wife addicted to travel—"I cannot see, Miss Tyroll, that the new milk can be so much better. Just look at the cows! I'm sure I've seen some at Hampstead twice the size; and as for condition! And then the bread again: how can we tell what stuff they put into it to make it white? At home, we know there's alum in it; and that's the worst of it, and all about it. But here, I never dare think about it. Miss Lambert is quite foolish about violets; and I don't deny it is very nice indeed to have them when you certainly could not in England, and I like them as well as anyone; but I don't know that it makes so much difference after all, in one's comfort, in the long-run."

"Certainly not," replied Miss Tyroll, who was a person of decisive mind and manners. "Foreign countries are much the best places for having things which you can very well do without; but, for my part, I like England best. Don't you get very tired of marble and pillars and church-bells? I do."

"So do I," assented Mrs. Bloxam; "and all the places one is obliged to go to are so large and bare." And then the two ladies discussed the subject just started at great length. Even the climate had little merit in the prejudiced estimation of Mrs. Bloxam. She had felt it quite as cold by the Arno as ever she had felt it by the Thames; and she thought the *tramontana* was only a piercing wind with a pretty name. She had felt very much the same sort of thing in London, where she could take refuge from it in a snug room with warm curtains and a coal fire.

She had no fancy for sitting with her feet baking over *braise*, and she had seen at Dulwich and Hampton Court pictures enough to satisfy all her aspirations after art. There was something educational in the way in which visitors to Florence —and, indeed, Gertrude herself—did the churches and the galleries which was rather oppressive to Mrs. Bloxam. She hated all that reminded her of the life of sordid toil she had lived through and freed herself from ; she did not like to learn anything, because she could not get rid of the feeling that by doing so she was exposing herself to the danger of having to teach it again. But all her personal discontent did not interfere with Mrs. Bloxam's interest in Gertrude, and did not render her an unpleasant companion. She was not sympathetic ; but Gertrude had been little used to sympathy, and she did not greatly care about it—it never interfered with her enjoyment of anything, that she had to enjoy it alone. She did all in her power to make Mrs. Bloxam's life comfortable and happy, and she never interrupted or withheld her assent from the frequent remini-

scences of Bayswater in which her friend indulged; but she liked her life in Italy, and she
entertained a strong conviction that, as she had
never been so happy before (for she had come to
regard the brief period of her love for Lloyd as
an interval of hallucination), so the future could
hardly bring her anything better. She had no
doubts, no fears about success in her adopted
profession. The favourable opinions which had
been pronounced by competent judges in England were confirmed and strengthened by those
to which she attached most value in Italy, and
her progress was surprising to herself and her in-
structors.

The correspondence between Mrs. Bloxam and
Lord Sandilands was frequent and *suivie*. Mrs.
Bloxam was a clever letter-writer, and the recipient of her epistles found in them a source
of interest which life had long lacked for him.
If the young lady in whom he had discovered
Gertrude Gautier's daughter had been merely
handsome, he would have been pleased with her,
doubtless would have taken a kindly interest in

her; had she been only clever he would have felt a secret pride in her talent, and watched its manifestations with a hidden interest : but she was both handsome and clever, and highly gifted; and all the feelings which, but for his own fault, he might once have declared and indulged openly, had been gratified to the fullest extent.

As time went on, the "working of the oracle" was done in London by the *impresario* and his assistants in a masterly fashion. The higher branch of the same industry was also conducted by the Marchioness of Carabas with all the success to which her ladyship was so well accustomed in her social manœuvrings. To such members of her coterie as understood her passionate devotion to art, her untiring exertions in its interests, and to its professors, she spoke in raptures of her "dear Grace Lambert," carefully avoiding the distant precision of the "Miss" and the too fond familiarity of the "Grace;" she read what she called "pet bits" of her young *protégée's* letters, which were neither numerous nor lengthy; predicted the future value of those

precious autographs, and contrived to keep a
flickering flame of interest in Grace Lambert
alive, which her appearance would readily blow
into a blaze. The steadiness of dear Lady Carabas to this "fancy," as her friends called it,
created some astonishment among her circle. She
was more remarkable for the vehemence than for
the duration of her attachments. It had happened to many aspirants for fame, or for social
success, or some other of the many objects which
people think worth attainment, even if a little
self-respect has to be sacrificed in the process,
to find themselves somehow unaccountably set
aside by Lady Carabas after a certain season of
favour—happily, sometimes, long enough to have
enabled them to extract from it all the profit
they desired : not " dropped"—that is a rude
proceeding, wanting in finesse, quite unworthy of
the Carabas *savoir faire*—but calmly, impercep-
tibly set aside; whereat the wise among the
number were amused, and the foolish were savage.
But Grace Lambert held her place even during
her absence. There was something captivating

to the fancy in the idea of the cultivation in "seclusion" of that great talent of which the world had got an inkling, under the auspices of Lady Carabas, and which would inevitably be a splendid testimony in the future to her judgment and taste. Thus, the way for her appearance and success in London being made plainer, easier, and pleasanter for her day by day, and the purpose of her sojourn in Italy fulfilled in a like ratio, time slipped away, and the period named for the return of Grace Lambert and Mrs. Bloxam—who hailed it with delight, and who now positively pined for Bayswater—drew near.

There had not been seen such a house at the Grand Scandinavian Opera for years; there had not been heard such long-continued thunders of applause, such rounds of cheering, since the Brödchen's *début*. Lady Carabas and Mr. Munns had each "worked the oracle," according to their lights; but the discrimination of her ladyship's friends rendered the managerial *claque* quite unnecessary. The opera was the *Trovatore,* and Gertrude's entrance as Leonora was the signal for a subdued murmur of applause. People were too anxious to see and hear her to give vent to any loud expression of their feelings; but when, with perfect composure, and without the smallest trace of nervousness in face or voice, the girl burst into the lovely "Tacea la notte," the connoisseurs knew that her success was accomplished; and long before the enthusiastic roar surged forth at the conclusion of the air Mr. Boulderson Munns, who had been nervously playing with the ends of his dyed moustache, shut up his opera-glass, and said to his treasurer and alter-ego, Mr. William Duff, "By ——, Billy, she'll smash the other shop!"

The lobbies and the refreshment-room were emptying of the crowds which had been raving to each other after the first act of the beauty and talent of the *débutante,* when Lord Ticehurst, who had been among the loudest demonstrators in the omnibus-box, whither he was returning, met Gilbert Lloyd quietly ascending the stairs.

"Only just come in?" asked his lordship.

"Only this instant; straight from Arlington-street; it's all right about Charon."

"O, d—n Charon!" said Lord Ticehurst; "you've missed the most splendid reception—Miss Grace Lambert, you know!"

"My dear fellow, I know nothing—except that Lady Carabas insisted on my going to her box to-night, to hear a new singer."

"There never was such a cold-blooded fish as you, Gilbert! Now be quick, and you'll be in time to see her come on in the second act!"

Gilbert Lloyd walked very leisurely to Lady Carabas' box on the grand tier, and received his snubbing for being late with due submission. When the roar of applause announced the re-appearance of the evening's heroine, he looked up still leisurely; but the next instant his glass was fixed to his eyes, and then his hand shook and his cheeks were even whiter than usual, and his nether-lip was firmly held by his teeth, as in Miss Grace Lambert, the successful *debutante*, he recognised his wife.

Book the Second.

CHAPTER I.

PROGRESS.

MR. BOULDERSON MUNNS was right in the remark which he made to his treasurer and *fidus Achates*, Mr. William Duff, in regard to Miss Grace Lambert's success, and to the effect which it would have on the future of the opposition opera-house. That very night the triumph was achieved. Ladies who "looked in for a minute" at various balls and receptions after the opera talked to each other of no one but the new singer; the smoking-rooms of the clubs rang with her praises. Schrink, the humpbacked critic of the *Statesman*, went off straight to the Albion in Drury-lane; called for some hot brandy-and-water and a pen and ink; seated himself in his accustomed box, into which no one else dared intrude, and dashed off something, which, when

it appeared in print the next morning, proved to
be an elaborate and scholarly eulogy of the new
singer. The other journals were equally lauda-
tory, and the result of the general commendation
was soon proved. The box-office was besieged
from morning till night; boxes and stalls were
taken for weeks in advance; crowds began to
collect round the pit and gallery doors at three
o'clock in the afternoon, and remained there, increasing in size and turbulence, until the doors
were opened; while the fugitive Miramella and
the recreant Jacowski were singing away for dear
life at the Regent Theatre, to empty benches.
The fact of Miss Lambert's being an English-
woman was with many people a great thing in
her favour. Old people who recollected Miss
Paton, and middle-aged people who still raved
about Miss Adelaide Kemble, hurried off to see
the young lady who had succeeded to the laurels
erst won so gallantly and worn so gracefully by
these two great English singers, and came back
loud in her praise. The *Mirror* — the weekly
journal of theatricals and music — uplifted its

honest, ungrammatical, kindly voice in favour of
the *débutante*, and gossipped pleasantly of Kitty
Stephens, Vestris, and the few other English-
women who have ever sung in time and tune.
The *Illustrated News* published Miss Lambert's
portrait on the same page with the portrait of the
trowel with which the Mayor of Mudfog had laid
the foundation-stone of the Mudfog Infirmary;
and the *Penny Woodcutter* reproduced the engraving which had previously done duty as
Warawaki, Queen of the Tonongo Islands, and
subscribed Miss Lambert's name to it. A very
gorgeous red-and-white engraving of the new
singer figured also on the "Grace Valse," inscribed to her by her obedient humble servant
Luigi Vasconi, who was leader of the orchestra
of Mr. Munns' establishment, and who played
first fiddle under the renowned conductor, Signor
Cocco; while the enterprising hosier in the Arcade under the opera-house produced a new style
of neck-tie which he christened "The Lambert,"
and of which he would probably have sold more
had the Arcade been anything of a thoroughfare.

As it was, the young man who kept the books of Messrs. Octave and Finings, the wine-merchants, and who was known to have plunged madly into love with the new singer when he went in once with a gallery-order, sported a " Lambert," and led the fashionable world of Lamb's - Conduit-street in consequence.

Was this fame ? It was notoriety, at all events. To have your portrait in all the photograph-shops and the illustrated journals; to see your name blazing in large type in every newspaper, and on every hoarding and dead-wall of London ; to read constant encomiastic mention of yourself in what are called, or miscalled, the organs of public opinion; to be pointed out by admiring friends to other admiring friends in the streets; to be the cynosure of crowds; to be the butt of the *Scarifier*—when some artist or contributor to that eminent journal has seen you on horseback while he was on foot, or seen you clean while he was dirty, or heard you praised while he was unnoticed—these are the recognitions of popularity received by art - workers, be they writers, or painters, or actors. Not very great, not very ennobling, perhaps, but pleasant—confess it, O my sisters and brethren in art! Pleasanter to earn hundreds by the novel, or the picture, or the acting—imperfect though each may be in its way—which shall cause thousands to think kindly of us, than to receive two guineas for verbal vitriol-throwing in the *Scarifier;* pleasanter than to stand up, earning nothing at all, to be howled at night after night by the vinous members of the opposite political party, and to be switched morning after morning by their press-organs; pleasanter than to go for forty years for six hours a day to the Tin-tax Office, and at last to arrive at six hundred a-year, with the chance of receiving a pension of two-thirds of the amount, if you prove by medical certificate that you are thoroughly worn out! That worn, gray old gentleman going in to enjoy the joint, and the table, and a pint of sherry at the Senior United, lost his youth and his hopes and his liver in India, and in a few years may perhaps get—just in time to leave it to his heir—the prize-money which he won a

quarter of a century ago; that Irish gentleman
with a chin-tuft has sold the last of his paternal
acres to carry him through his third election, and
may possibly obtain from the Government, which
he has always earnestly supported, a commission-
ership of five hundred a-year. We can do better
than that, we others! So, let us say, with the
French actress, " *Qu'on leur donne des grimaces
pour leur argent et vivons heureux!*" and in a
modified and anglicised sense, " *Vive la vie de
Bohème!*"

Did Gertrude care much for this kind of cheap
incense burnt in her honour? Truth to tell, she
cared for it very little indeed. When she accepted the stage instead of the concert-room for
her career, she was influenced, as we have seen,
by an idea of the brilliancy of her triumph,
should she succeed; but that triumph once secured, there was an end to such feeling in the
matter, so far as she was personally concerned.
She took it all in a perfectly business-like manner; it was good, she supposed, for the theatre
that she had succeeded. Gratified? O yes, of

course, she was gratified; but when people came
and told her there had never been anything heard
like her, she was compelled to show them that, in
accepting professional singing for her livelihood,
she had not quite abnegated any pretension to common sense. With the exception of devoting the
necessary time to rehearsals and study, her time
was spent very much as it was before her departure to Italy. The drawing-room of the little
Bayswater villa was gorgeous and fragrant with
anonymous bouquets, offerings left the previous
night at the stage-door; but Miss Lambert had
not made one single new acquaintance since the
night of her *début*. Occasionally on "off-nights"
she would be seen at Carabas House, or at one or
two of the other houses which she had been in the
habit of visiting before the commencement of her
professional career; but though she was inundated
with invitations, she steadfastly refused to increase
her visiting-list; and the lion-hunters, male and
female, in vain sought to get her to their houses,
and equally in vain sought admittance to hers.

To none was she a greater enigma than to her

manager, Mr. Boulderson Munns. Proud of her success, and disposed in his open-hearted vulgarity to testify to her his appreciation of it, that liberal gentleman purchased a gaudy and expensive diamond-bracelet, had an appropriate inscription in gilt letters put on to its morocco-leather case, and sent it to Miss Grace Lambert. The next morning, bracelet, case and all were laid on the managerial table, with a little note from Miss Lambert thanking Mr. Munns very sincerely for his kindness, but declining the present on the grounds that Miss Lambert was doing no more than fulfilling the terms of her engagement, and adding, that if Mr. Munns had found that engagement profitable, the time to show his appreciation of it would be when they came to settle terms for the next season. There was a combination of independence and business in this reply, which tickled Mr. Munns exceedingly. At first he was annoyed at the note, read it with a portentous frown, and strode up and down his room, plucking at the dyed whiskers wrathfully. But by the time Mr. Duff arrived with his usual budget of letters to be read, bills to be paid, questions to be asked, &c., the great *impresario* had softened down wonderfully, and had forgotten his rage at what he at first imagined the slight put upon him by his new singer, in his impossibility to comprehend her.

"I can't make her out, Billy," said he, "and that's the fact. I've known 'em of all kinds; but she licks the lot. Look here at her letter! She won't have that bracelet, Billy—just shove it into the strong-box, will you? we can get the inscription altered, and it'll do for somebody else—and talks about fresh terms for next season. Reg'lar knowing little shot, ain't she? Quiet little devil, too; wouldn't come down to my garden-party at Teddington, on Wednesday, though I had the Dook and Sir George, and a whole lot of 'em dyin' to be introduced to her. 'No go, your Grace!' I said, 'she won't come; but when Venus is bashful let's stick to Bacchus, who's always our friend.' I haven't had a classical education, Billy, but I think that was rather neat; and so they did, and punished the 'sham' awfully. However, it's all good for trade. She and that old cat, her aunt

—not her aunt? well, Bloxam; you know who I mean—go about to Lady Carabas', and all the right sort of people, and the more she won't know the wrong sort of people, the more they want to know her, and the 'let's' tremendous. The other shop's done up, sir; chawed up, smashed! Mac-Bone and Ivory and Déloge, and the rest of 'em, tell me they can't sell a stall for the Regent; and I hear that Miramella threatened Jacowski with a fork at dinner the other day, because he spoke of Miss Lambert, and swore she'd go to America. Best thing she could do, stupid old fool!"

Although this feeling in regard to Miss Lambert was perhaps nowhere expressed in language so strongly symbolical as that used by Mr. Munns, there is no doubt that it was generally felt. There is a certain class of artist-patronising society which has the *mot d'ordre* of the *siffleur's* box, and revels in the gossip of the *coulisses*. These worthy persons were in the habit of talking to each other constantly of the new *prima donna*—how she came in "a regular fly, my dear;" how she was always dressed in black silk, "made quite plain, and

rather dowdy;" how she was always accompanied
by the same old lady, who, whether at rehearsal
or in the evening, never left her side; and how,
with the exception of Lord Sandilands, with whom
she seemed to be very intimate, she entered into
conversation with no one during the performance;
—in all which things Miss Grace Lambert dif-
fered very much from Madame Miramella, who—
depending on the kind of temper in which she
might happen to be—alternated between the most
gorgeous garments and the most miserable *chif-
fons;* between a coroneted brougham with a five-
hundred-guinea pair of horses, and a four-wheeler
cab; between the loveliest complexion, and the
most battered old parchment mask; between the
most queenlike courtesy to all around her in the
theatre, and the use of French and Italian *argot-*
abuse, which fortunately was incomprehensible to
those to whom it was addressed. In this society
Lord Sandilands was far too well-known for the
smallest breath of scandal ever to attach to Miss
Lambert's name by reason of his intimacy with
her. People remembered how devoted he had

been to the Rossignol—who died, poor lady, in the height of her success—who had the voice of an angel, and the face of a little sheep; how he had fought an uphill fight for Miss Laverock until he had seen her properly ranked in her profession; how he had always been the kind and disinterested friend of musical talent. They wondered that somebody else did not arrive, some English duke, some Italian prince, some *millionnaire*, and bear her away as Madame Sontag, Miss Chester, Miss Stephens, and Madame Duvernay had been borne away before her. She was "thoroughly proper, my dear," they told each other in confidence; and the obvious result of propriety being marriage, they waited for that result with great impatience.

The successful *début* of the young lady whom the world regarded as his *protégée*, but whom he in his secret soul acknowledged as his daughter, had given Lord Sandilands unmitigated satisfaction. Unmitigated, because his worldly knowledge had given him sufficient insight into Gertrude's character to enable him to perceive that she could ride in safety over billows and through tempests in which a less evenly-ballasted bark would inevitably suffer shipwreck; to perceive that the triumph which she had achieved would leave her head unturned; while in the position which she had gained, her heart would be just as much at her command as it was when she first surprised society in the drawing-room of Carabas House. So, thoroughly happy, the old nobleman permeated society, listening with eager ears to all comments on Miss Grace Lambert. He heard them everywhere. Steady old boys at the Portland had heard of the new singer from their "people," and intended, the first evening they had to spare, to make one in the family-box, and hear her. Fast men, young and old, at the Arlington, relaxing their great minds—*neque arcum semper tendit Apollo*—between turf-talk and whist-playing, spoke of her in exaggerated laudation. In many of the houses where he had formerly been accustomed to drop in with tolerable regularity, he had renewed the habit since Gertrude's arrival in London; pleasant, genial, hospitable houses, all the more genial that neither

frisky matrons, nor foolish virgins, nor gilded
youth, were to be reckoned among the component parts of the society to be found in them;
and there he found that Miss Lambert was uni-
versally popular. A very great lady indeed—one
who held herself, and, truth to tell, was generally
held, far above the Carabas set, or any other of
the kind — no less a lady than the Dowager
Duchess of Broadwater — wrote to Lord Sandilands, saying that she had heard very much of
Miss Lambert, and hoping that through Lord
Sandilands' influence the young lady might be
induced to come and see an old woman who never
went out. If you have studied polite society and
its Bible—the Peerage—you will know that the
dowager duchess is the widow of that good, kind
duke who was nothing more than the best landlord, and the most perfectly representative English nobleman of his time; who reduced the rents
of his tenants, and built model cottages for his
labourers, and loved music next to his wife, and
composed pretty little pieces, which were played
with much applause at the Ancient Concerts. A

stately gentleman, tall, clean shaven, with his
white hair daintily arranged, with his blue coat,
buff waistcoat, and tight gray trousers in the
morning; his *culotte courte*, black-silk stockings,
and buckled shoes in evening attire. His son,
the present duke, wears a rough red beard,
buys his frieze shooting-coat and sixteen-shilling
trousers from a cheap tailor, smokes a short pipe,
and talks like a stable-man. His mother, who
adores him—he adores her, let us confess, and
is as soft and docile with her as when he was
a child—looks at him wonderingly; she is of the
vieille cour, and cannot understand the "lowering"
tone of the present day. *Grande dame* as she is,
she relaxes always towards the professors of that
art which her husband so loved; and when Miss
Lambert was brought to her by Lord Sandilands, and sang two little convent-airs which the
old lady recollected having heard, ah, how many
years ago! she drew the girl towards her, and
with streaming eyes kissed her forehead, and
bade her thank God for the great talent which
He had bestowed upon her, and which ought

always to be used in His service. After that interview, Gertrude saw a great deal of the old duchess, who always received her with the greatest affection, and introduced her to the small circle of intimate acquaintances by which she was surrounded.

And Lady Carabas, who was necessarily apprised of all that happened in Grace Lambert's life, was by no means annoyed at or jealous of her *protégée's* introduction to the Dowager Duchess of Broadwater, of whom, in truth, her ladyship stood somewhat in awe; not that she ever confessed this for an instant, speaking of her always as a " most charming person," and " quite the nicest old lady of the day;" but having at the same time an inward feeling that the " charming person," though always perfectly polite, did not reciprocate the respect which Lady Carabas professed, and, indeed, really felt for her. The dowager duchess's society was as rigidly exclusive as Lady Carabas' was decidedly mixed; and the platonic *liaisons* into which the Marchioness's Soul was always leading her were regarded with

very stony glances from under very rigid eyebrows by the Broadwater faction. Lady Carabas
had somewhat more than a dim idea of all this,
and had quite sufficient sense of the fitness of
things to be aware that it was more politic in
her to accept the position than to fight against
it—to know that for a recognised *protégée* of hers
to be received by the Broadwater clique tacitly
reflected credit on her; and so, while she shrug-
ged her shoulders when she heard of Lady
Lowndes, and undisguisedly expressed her scorn
at the attempts made by other lion-hunters to
get hold of Gertrude, she warmly congratulated
Lord Sandilands on the Broadwater connection,
and redoubled her praises of Miss Lambert's voice
and virtues. These laudations, skilfully served,
as a woman of Lady Carabas' worldly experience alone knows how to express them, were
always well received by the old nobleman, who
could not hear too much in Gertrude's favour,
and who day by day felt himself growing fonder
of her, and more thoroughly associated with her
plans and her welfare.

And there was one other person to whom this lady was equally enchanting, who never wanted the song pitched in any other key, who listened in rapt delight so long as he was allowed to listen and gaze and dream—Miles Challoner, who had left town so soon as he found the pretty Bayswater villa deserted, on Gertrude's departure for Italy. He had no further tie to London, and cared not to remain haunting the neighbourhood of the nest whence his "bird with the shining head" had fled. He became suddenly convinced of the utter emptiness of metropolitan existence, and expatiated thereon to Lord Sandilands in a way which greatly amused the old nobleman. He declared that these nineteenth-century views of life were false and wrongly based; that half the vices and shortcomings of the provincial poor and the labouring classes were due to the absenteeism of the landlords, who by example should lead their inferiors. The holder of an estate, Miles said, be it small or large, had duties which should keep him among his people. He felt that he had neglected these duties; and though he was not specially cut for a country gentleman's life, he knew that he ought to go down to Rowley Court, and do his best to get on in that sphere of life to which he had been called. The young man said all this with great earnestness, for at the moment he really believed it; and he was half-inclined to be angry when Lord Sandilands, who had listened to the rhapsody with a grave and attentive face, could contain himself no longer, but broke into a smile as he said that he thought Miles perfectly right, "particularly as the shooting-season was coming on." So Miles left London, and went to his old ancestral home. The bright bountiful beauty of summer still decked the woods and fields; the old servants and the villagers vied with each other in welcoming the young squire; and Miles felt that he had done rightly in following what he was pleased to call the dictates of his conscience, in coming back. The small sum of money which he had expended on the estate had been judiciously laid out, and improvement was manifest everywhere—in heavy crops, mended fences, and common land drained and reclaimed;

in repaired outhouses, and shooting properly pre-
served; and, better than all, in a higher class of
tenantry, and larger rents. Miles Challoner had
never felt the pleasant sense of proprietorship
until this visit to his home. He walked round
his fields, he stood on little vantage-points and
surveyed his estate, with an inward feeling of
pride which he did not care to check. It *was*
something to be an English country gentleman,
after all. He had been nothing and no one in
London, a hanger-on, a unit in the great social
stream—no better than a dancing barrister, or a
flirting clerk in a government office; two-thirds
of the people he visited knowing his name, and
that he had been properly introduced to them
by some accountable person, but nothing more.
While here, he was the young squire; as he
passed, the " hat was plucked from the slavish
villager's head;" everybody knew him, and was
anxious to be seen by him; he was the man of
the place, and—Yes, it would not be difficult to
make out one's life in that position; not as a
bachelor, of course, but provided he had someone

with him. Someone? No difficulty in finding
her! If he knew the language of laughing eyes,
Emily Walbrook would not object to become
the mistress of Rowley Court. And with her
father Sir Thomas's money what might not be
done? The old place might be rehabilitated,
the lost lands recovered, the old dignity of the
family restored.

But Miles Challoner, being a gentleman
and not an adventurer, told himself, after very
little self-examination, that he did not care
for Miss Walbrook, and that he never could
care for her, consequently that he would be a
scoundrel to think of proposing for her hand;
told himself further that he only did care and
only had cared—apart from some boyish follies
which had not done him nor anyone else any
harm—for one person in the world, Grace Lambert. Did she care for him? He did not know;
but, honestly, he thought she did not. And if
she did, should he bring her there, to Rowley
Court, as his wife? Did he care for her sufficiently to suffer the universal inquiries as to who

she was, the generally uplifted eyebrows and supercilious remarks when the reply was given? At present she was only known as a young lady received in excellent society on account of her musical talents; but if this report was true— this report that she had gone to Italy with the intention of perfecting herself as a singer on the operatic stage? A singer? The stage? The general and only notion of the stage in the neighbourhood of Rowley Court was founded on reminiscences of the travelling troupe of mummers who had once or twice come to Bleakholme Fair; poor half-starved creatures, who had performed a dismal tragedy in an empty barn, by the light of a hoop of guttering tallow candles. How could he prepare the Bœotian mind of Gloucestershire to receive as his wife a woman who would bring with her such associations as these? What would be said by the old county neighbours, by whom the old Challoner name was yet held in the highest respect and regard? What by the wealthy new-comers, whose influence was day by day increasing, and who gave themselves airs of pride and position and exclusiveness far more intolerable than the loftiest hauteur of the real territorial *seigneurie?* Poor Miles! and after all—even if he had made up his mind to brave all the outcry that might arise; to say, " I love this woman, and I bestow on her my rank and my position; accept her as my wife, or leave her alone; think as you please, talk as you please, and go to the deuce!"—he was by no means certain that Miss Grace Lambert would see the magnitude of the sacrifice he was making for her, or, indeed, that she would have anything to say to him.

That was a dull winter for Miles Challoner, that duty season when he steadfastly went through the character of the English country gentleman, to the tolerable satisfaction of his neighbours and his tenants, but to his own intense disgust. He hunted twice a week, he shot constantly; he attended church regularly, and kept rigidly awake during the dear old vicar's dull sermons; he gave two or three dull bachelor dinners, where the vicar, the curate, little Dr. Barford, and two or

three neighbouring fox-hunting squires, ate and
drank, and prosed wearily for three or four hours;
and he went out occasionally. He dined with
Lord Boscastle, the lord-lieutenant and principal
grandee of the county, where he met all "the
best people," but where his attention was principally concentrated on his hostess; for Lady
Boscastle was *née* Amelia Milliken, and, as Amelia
Milliken, had been the great attraction for two
seasons at the Theatre Royal Hatton Garden,
during the lesseeship of the great Wuff. Miles
could hardly realise to himself that the mild,
elegant, dried-up, farinaceous-looking old lady
had been the incomparable actress who, as he
had heard his father relate, entered so thoroughly
into her art that she would shed real scalding
tears upon the stage; and whose Juliet yet remained in the memory of old playgoers as the
most perfect impersonation ever witnessed. She
was an actress when Lord Boscastle married her;
and see her now, with a cabinet minister on her
right hand, and the best families of the county
honoured by her intercourse! Why could not he

do the same with Grace Lambert? And then Miles recollected that he was not so great a man as Lord Boscastle, had not the same weight and *prestige;* remembered also that he had heard his father say that Lady Boscastle made her way very slowly into the county society; that she had an immense number of disagreeables to contend with at first; and that it was only the sweet-. ness of her disposition, and her wonderful patience and forbearance, that carried her through. And though Miles Challoner was undoubtedly in love with Miss Lambert, he scarcely thought that sweetness of disposition, patience, and long-suffering were the virtues in which she specially excelled. Miles also dined with Sir Thomas Walbrook, where there was much more display and formality than at Lord Boscastle's—only that the display was in bad taste, and the formality betokened ill-breeding; and he went to a hunt-ball, and tried to attend the weekly meetings of a whist-club, but broke down in the attempt. In the daytime he did not fare so badly, for he was full of life and health, and the love for field-sports

which had distinguished him when a boy came
back renewed when he again joined in those
sports; but in the long evenings he moped and
moaned, and was dreadfully bored.

The fact is that, however much he endeavoured to persuade himself to the contrary, he
was in love with Miss Grace Lambert; and the
more persistently he turned his thoughts from
that young lady, the more he found himself
taking interest in persons and things associated
with her. He corresponded regularly with Lord
Sandilands, and his every letter contained some
inquiry after or allusion to "your young friend
in Italy." The old nobleman chuckled over the
frequency and the tone of these letters, but replied
to them regularly, and invariably said something
about Grace; something, too, which he thought
would please the recipient of the letter, for he
loved Miles with fatherly affection; and, if Gertrude saw fit, nothing would have pleased him
better than that the two young people should
make a match of it. That, however, was entirely
for Gertrude to determine; and nothing could

come of it yet, at all events, as she had the stage
career before her. Meantime, there was no reason
why pleasant reports of her progress should not
go down to Rowley Court. And when Miles received the letters, he ran his eye over them hurriedly to see where *the* name appeared, and read
those bits first, and re-read them, and then dropped
very coolly and leisurely into the perusal of his
old friend's gossip.

He was a queer, odd fellow, though, this Miles
Challoner; full of that dogged determination which
we call "British," and are extremely proud of
(though, like the man who "treated resolution,"
in the end we often do the thing which we have
so stubbornly refused to do); and although he
knew that Miss Lambert had returned, and was
about making her *début* in public, he remained
stationary at Rowley Court. He received letters
regularly from Lord Sandilands, but none of them
ever contained a hint or a suggestion that he
should come up to town; indeed, Miles guessed
that Miss Lambert would be far too much occupied to admit of his seeing her, and he had

said he would "give that up"—"that" being
the guiding motive of his life—and he would hold
to it. So Miles Challoner was not in the Grand
Scandinavian Opera-house on the night when
Gertrude made her triumphal entry into theatrical life. But when, the next day, he read the
flaming accounts of her success in the newspapers; when he received letters from Lord
Sandilands and other friends, filled with ravings
about her voice, her beauty, and her elegance;
when he felt that this fresh flame would
enormously increase the circle of her admirers,
many of whom might have the chance—which
they would not neglect as he was neglecting it
— of personal acquaintance with her, — he
could withstand the influence no longer, but
made immediate arrangements for returning to
London.

His old friend received him with his accustomed warmth, talked about the length of time he
had been away, and rallied him on the probable
cause of his detention. "I know, my dear boy!"
said Lord Sandilands; "I know all about what

you're going to tell me,—the pleasure a man feels in his own *terre;* the delightful days you used to have with Sir Peter's pack; the unequalled cover-shooting, and all the rest of it. Those things don't keep a young man down in the country, leading that frightful dead-alive existence which we try to think pleasant. I know all about it; and I know that there's nothing more horrible. There must be *beaux yeux* somewhere, when a man voluntarily accepts that kind of life; and, by Jove! it's a kind of life to make one find the most ordinary eyes *beaux.* That confounded country life has produced more *mésalliances,* and more—hem! What are you going to do with yourself to-day?" The old nobleman stopped his discourse abruptly, with the reflection, per-haps, that *mésalliances* scarcely fitted him for a theme. Answering him, Miles said that he had nothing to do, and that he was entirely at his friend's disposal.

"Then," said Lord Sandilands, "suppose we stroll out Bayswater way? You have not seen Miss Lambert for a long time now, though you know—for I wrote to you, and you must have heard in a hundred other places—of her success. Really, the greatest thing for years. Everybody enchanted; and, best of all, has not made the smallest difference in her; just the same un-affected, quiet, unpretending girl as when we met her that first night—don't you recollect?— at Carabas House."

They walked across Kensington-gardens and speedily reached the byeroad in which Miss Lambert's pretty villa was situated. Up and down this road, fretting against the slowness of the pace allowed them, stepping grandly, and sending the foam in flying flakes around them, were a pair of horses in a handsome mail-phaeton, driven by a correctly-appointed groom.

" Mr. Munns here!" said Lord Sandilands testily, as this sight broke upon him. " Horribly vexing, when we hoped to have the young lady all to ourselves, eh, Miles? A worthy man, Mr. Munns, but a dreadful vulgarian. Tell me, is it my short-sightedness, or has this fellow really mounted a cockade in his man's hat?"

"There certainly is a cockade in the man's hat," said Miles, with a smile which died away as, on a nearer approach, he added, "and a coronet on the harness."

"A coronet? Why, the man can never have been ass enough to—eh? O dear me, impossible! Who's phaeton's that, sir, eh?"

"Earl of Ticehurst's, my lord!" said the groom, touching his hat; "lordship's in there, my lord," pointing to the villa with his whip, "with her ladyship."

"With her ladyship!" echoed Lord Sandilands in bewilderment. "Let us go in, Miles, and see what it all means."

They saw what it all meant when they found Lady Carabas talking about education to Mrs. Bloxam in the drawing-room, and saw Lord Ticehurst walking with Miss Lambert round the little garden. Lord Sandilands frowned very gloomily, but Lady Carabas made straight at him. She had been dying to see dear Miss Lambert; she wanted so to see how she bore her success — ah, what a success! — and how charming she is over it all! not changed in the smallest degree. And her own horses were regularly knocked up with all their work just now; and as it was such a long way (fashionable people think anything west of Apsley House or north of Park-lane quite out of bounds), she had asked her nephew Etchingham to drive her over. Lord Sandilands bowed very grimly, and Miles Challoner then came forward. Lady Carabas was enchanted to see him; rallied him on his absence on the night of the *debut;* hoped to have him constantly at Carabas House, and was overwhelmingly gracious. Then Lord Ticehurst and Gertrude came in, and after a few conventional remarks, the young patrician, after a casual glance out of the window, informed his aunt that "the chestnuts had already stamped up the road into a regular ploughed field, by Jove! and that, as the parish would probably send in the paving-bill, perhaps the best thing they could do was to be off;" and accordingly he and Lady Carabas retired, with many adieux.

When they were gone, Lord Sandilands approached Gertrude and congratulated her with mock solemnity on her new acquaintance. "You have achieved an earl, my dear child, and there is no saying now to what you may not aspire. Charles the Fifth picking up Titian's pencil will be equalled by Lord Ticehurst's turning over the leaves of your music-book for you. Or in time we might get a duke to—"

"We want no higher member of the peerage than a baron, apparently, to render his order ridiculous," said Gertrude, turning upon him with a sarcastic bow and a little *moue*. "Don't be angry, dear friend," she continued; "but I own I cannot stand raillery where Lord Ticehurst is concerned. I have no doubt he means well—I am sure of it; all he says is genuine, and, so far as he can make it, polite; but he is very silly and very slangy, and—I can't endure him. — And now, Mr. Challoner, tell me of all your doings during your long absence in the country."

Lord Sandilands had a great deal to say to Mrs. Bloxam on the subject of any future visits which Lord Ticehurst might wish to pay to the Bayswater villa, and said it pointedly, and without circumlocution. When he rejoined the young people, he found them deep in conversation, and Miles, at least, looking very happy.

CHAPTER II.

INTEGRATIO AMORIS.

WHEN Gilbert Lloyd satisfied himself that the new opera-singer, at whose most successful *debut* he had " assisted," was none other than his wife, the momentary agitation which had so shaken him passed away, and he sat himself down at the back of Lady Carabas' box—not in the chair usually reserved for the controller for the time being of the Soul, but in a more retired position—and gave himself up, as any uninterested auditor might have done, to listening to the singing. He had never been particularly fond of music, and though he had always known that his wife possessed a fine voice, and had even at one time taken into consideration the probable profits which would accrue were he to *exploiter* her musical talent, he had never imagined the possibility of her taking such a position as that in which he now found her. Gilbert Lloyd was a man who believed thoroughly in the truth of that axiom which tells us that "there is a time for everything;" it would be quite time enough for him to analyse the new light which had been let into his life, to weigh and balance the pros and cons connected with the appearance of Gertrude on a scene which he was accustomed to tread, mixed up with people with whom he was to a certain extent familiar; it would be time enough for him to enter into those business details on the next morning, when his brain would be fresh and clear, and he would be recruited by his night's rest, and able more clearly to see his way, and arrive at a more accurate decision as to the advisability of steps to be taken. Meanwhile, he would listen with the rest; and he did listen, with great pleasure, joining heartily in the applause, and delighting Lady Carabas by the warmth of his outspoken admiration of her favourite. And he escorted her ladyship to her carriage; and went to the club, and played half-a-dozen rubbers with admirable coolness and self-posses-

sion. It was one of Gilbert Lloyd's strongest
points that he could put aside anything unpleasant
that might be pressing upon him, no matter how
urgently, and defer it for future consideration. In
the midst of trouble of all kinds—pecuniary com-
plications, turf anxieties, on the issue of which his
position in life depended—he would, after looking
at them vigorously with all his power, turn into
bed and sleep as calmly as though his mind were
entirely free, rising the next morning with renewed
health and courage to tackle the difficulties again.
Just at this period of Miss Lambert's *début*, Lloyd
happened to be particularly busy; the Derby—on
which he and his party were even more than
usually interested—was close at hand, and all
Gilbert's time was absorbed in "squaring" Lord
Ticehurst's book and his own. But he knew that
he need be under no alarm from the new element
in his life which had just cropped out: though he
had seen Gertrude, she had not seen him; there
was no reason as yet why they should be thrown
together; and even if they were, he was too fully
aware of her coldness and her pride to imagine

she would for an instant attempt to thrust herself
upon him, or even acknowledge him. So Gilbert
Lloyd made no difference in his life, beyond noting the name under which his wife was charming
the public, and paying attention whenever that
name was pronounced in his presence. He heard
all that—as we know—people said about her;
but as that all was praise of her public performance, and astonishment at the quietude of her
private life, it caused him very little emotion, and
that little of no pleasurable kind.

It was the intervening week between Epsom
and Ascot, and the season was at its height. The
Ticehurst party, thanks to the astute generalship
of Gilbert Lloyd, had pulled through the Derby
very well. Lord Ticehurst's horse had not won—
no one had ever imagined that possible—but it
had been brought up to such a position in the
betting as to secure the money for the stable, and
save its owner's credit with the public. Matters
for the future looked promising. To be sure, Lord
Ticehurst had not taken so much interest of late
in his turf speculations; but that did not particu-

larly affect Mr. Lloyd. So long as his patron
kept up his stud, and left the entire management
of everything to him, that gentleman was content.
It was not unnatural that a man of Lord Ticehurst's youth and health and position should wish
to enjoy himself in society; and Gilbert rather
encouraged his pupil's new notions on this point.
It was not that Orson was endowed with reason,
but rather that Orson had found out some *jeux
innocens* for himself, of which he did not require
his keeper's constant supervision.

One morning in the above-named week, Gilbert Lloyd was sitting in his own room in Lord
Ticehurst's bachelor-house in Hill-street. It was a
pleasant room on the first floor, and was furnished
in a manner half-substantial and half-pretty. The
large oak writing-table in the centre, the two or
three japanned deed-boxes on the floor, the hand-
ful of auctioneers' bills pinned to the wall, announcing property to be disposed of at forthcoming
sales—all these looked like business; but they were
diametrically contradicted by the cigar-boxes, the
pipe-rack, the Reynolds proofs, and the Pompeian

photographs on the walls; the ivory statuettes and the china monsters on the chimney-piece; the deer-skins and the tiger-skins, the heavy bronzes, the velvet *portières*, and the luxurious chairs and ottomans; all of which indicated the possession of good taste and the means of gratifying it. Gilbert Lloyd had chosen these rooms—his bedchamber adjoined his sitting-room—when the *ménage* was first transplanted to Hill-street from Limmer's— where, during the reign of Plater Dobbs, Lord Ticehurst had resided—and had kept them ever since. He had chosen them because they were pleasant and airy, and so far out of the way, that the ribald friends of the real proprietor—who were dropping into their companion's rooms on the ground-floor at all hours of the day and night— never thought of ascending to them. Trainers and jockeys made their way up the stairs with much muttered cursing, hating the ascent, which was troublesome to their short legs, and hating the business which brought them there; for Mr. Lloyd had a sharp tongue, and knew how to use it; and if his orders were not carried out to the letter, so

much the worse for those who had to obey them.
And latterly, a different class of visitors found
their way to Gilbert's room, demure attorneys and
portly land-agents; for Mr. Lloyd was now recognised as Lord Ticehurst's factotum; and all
matters connected with the estates, whether as
regards sale, purchase, or mortgage, passed
through his hands.

It was twelve o'clock in the day, and Gilbert
was seated at the oak writing-table. A banker's
pass-book lay open at his right hand, and he was
busied with calculations on a paper before him,
when there was a knock at the door, and upon the
cry "come in," Lord Ticehurst entered the room.
Gilbert looked up from his writing, and on seeing
who was his visitor, gave a short laugh.

"Won't you send up a servant with your
name, next time?" said he; "the idea of a man
knocking at a door in his own house—at least,
when that isn't the door of his wife's room! Then,
I've heard it's advisable to knock or cough outside,
or something of that sort, just to keep all straight,
you know!"

"Funny dog!" said Lord Ticehurst, indolently dropping into an easy-chair and puffing at his cigar. "How are you?"

"Well, but worried," answered Gilbert.

"That goes without saying," said his lordship; "you always are worried, or you would never be well!"

"Look here, Etchingham," exclaimed Gilbert Lloyd, with a mock air of intense interest, "you mustn't do this, 'pon my soul you mustn't, or you'll hurt yourself. I've noticed lately a distinct tendency on your part to be epigrammatic; you weren't intended for it, and it won't agree with you. Take a friend's advice, and cut it."

"Considerate old boy! Tell me the news."

"Tell *you* the news?—I like that. Tell the news to a man whose life is passed in what the newspaper fellows call the 'vortex of fashion;' who is so much engaged that his humble servant here can't get five minutes with him on business, when it's most particularly wanted. Tell *you* the news, indeed!"

"No. But I say, you know what I mean,

Gilbert. How are we getting on? Ascot, you know, and all that?"

"O, business! Well, Bosjesman will win the Trial Stakes, and Plume will be beaten like a sack for the Cup; both of which facts are good for us. We shall get Dumfunk's Derby-money, or most of it; he's come to terms—nice terms—with that discount company at Shrewsbury; and little Jim Potter's shoulder's better, and he'll be able to ride."

"And what about the house?"

"What house? Parliament? Does your lordship intend to put me in for Etchingham? I'm as fit as a fiddle for that work, and could roll them speeches off the reel—"

"Don't be an ass, Gilbert! I mean the house for the week—at Ascot?"

"O, I see! Yes, that's all settled. I couldn't get anything nearer than Windsor; but I've got a very pretty little box there. Charley Chesterton rents it for the year—he's there with the Blues, you know; but Mrs. Chesterton's going away, and Charley will go into barracks for the week, and we can have the house. It's a stiffish figure, but they can get any amount that week, you know."

"O yes, of course, that don't matter. And it's a nice house, you say?"

"Very pretty little place indeed—do very well for us."

"Yes. And Mrs. Chesterton's been living there? She's a nice woman, ain't she?"

"Yes, she's nice enough, as women go. But what has she to do with it?"

"Well—I mean to say, it's a sort of crib that—don't you know—one could ask a lady to stop in?"

"O—h!" exclaimed Gilbert Lloyd, with a very long face—"that's it, is it?"

"No, no, 'pon my soul, you don't understand what I mean," said Lord Ticehurst hurriedly. "Fact of the matter is, Lady Carabas wants to come down for the Cup-day; and she'll bring a friend, of course; and I told her about my having a house somewhere in the neighbourhood for the week, and thought she and the other lady, and

their maids and people, could—don't you see?—
stay. What do you think?"

"My dear Etchingham, whatever you wish,
of course shall be carried out. It is not for me
to teach etiquette to any lady, especially to Lady
Carabas, who despises conventionality, and who,
besides, is quite old enough to take care of herself. I should have thought that for a lady to
come to a bachelor's house—however, of course
she'll have her maid and her footman, and some
one to act as her *âme damnée*—her sheep-dog.
Who is the sheep-dog, by the way?"

"I don't know about sheep-dog," said Lord
Ticehurst, flushing very red; "but Lady Carabas
said the lady she proposed to do me the honour
to bring to my house was—was Miss Grace Lambert."

Gilbert Lloyd looked up without the smallest
trace of perturbation, and said, "Miss Grace
Lambert? O, the—the celebrated singer! O,
indeed!"

"Yes," said Lord Ticehurst; "there's a
chance of her getting a holiday on Thursday

night—town will be very empty, you know, and I think I shall be able to square it with Munns —and then she might come down to the races, and she and Lady Carabas could come over here afterwards. She's a most charming person, Gilbert."

"Is she?" said Gilbert Lloyd very slowly. "I have not—what you seem to have—the pleasure of her acquaintance. Have you known her long?"

"O, ever so long; ever since she first came out at a concert at Carabas House one night. Don't you recollect my pointing out to you a very stunning girl in a brougham, just as we were turning into Tatt's one day?"

"My dear fellow, you've pointed me out so many stunning girls when we've been turning into Tatt's, or elsewhere, that I really cannot distinguish that bright particular star. But I've seen Miss Lambert at the Opera."

"And she's a stunner, ain't she?"

"She seemed to be perfectly good-looking and lady-like on the stage. But these people are so different in private life."

"My dear Gilbert, I've seen her in private life, as you call it, a dozen times, and she's awfully nice."

"O, and she's awfully nice, eh?"

"What a queer fish you are! Of course she's awfully nice; and this place of Charley Chesterton's will do for these ladies to come to?'

"Yes, I should think so. Mrs. Chesterton is a woman accustomed to have the right thing about her; and it's good enough for her, so I presume it will 'do' for Miss Lambert and Lady Carabas."

"I hate you when you've got this sneering fit on you, Gilbert," said his lordship sulkily; and Gilbert Lloyd saw that he had gone far enough. His patron was wonderfully good-tempered, but, like all good-tempered men, when once put out, he "cut up rough" for a very long time.

"Don't be angry, Etchingham;" and Lloyd rose and crossed the room, and put his hand on the young man's shoulder. "I was only chaffing; and I was a little annoyed, perhaps, because you seemed doubtful whether this house that I have got, and only got after a great deal of trouble, would suit you. You might have depended on me. Well, and so you have made this young lady's acquaintance, and you find her charming?"

"Quite charmin'," said Lord Ticehurst, his good-humour being restored. "I've been with Lady Carabas several times to see her at a pretty little place she's got out Bayswater way, where she lives with an old tabby—by the way, I'll bet odds that old tabby don't let her come here without her."

"Well, there's room for the old tabby," said Gilbert. "But, see, Etchingham; do I really understand that you—that you care for this girl?"

"D—n it, Gilbert, you press a fellow home! Well, then, I'm not given to this sort of thing, as you know very well; but this time it's an awful case of spoons."

"Ah!" said Gilbert, smiling quietly, "your expression is slangy but vigorous. And what are your views with regard to her?"

"Jove!" said Lord Ticehurst, "only one way there, my dear fellow! Wouldn't stand any nonsense; any of 'em, I mean,—Lady Carabas and all that lot. Besides, she's a lady, you know—educated, and all that sort of thing; and as to looks and breedin', she could hold her own with any of 'em—eh?"

"Of course she could. Besides, chaff apart, when the Earl of Ticehurst chooses to marry, his countess—however, there's time enough to talk about that. Now run along, for I must write off at once about this Windsor house; and I've a heap of things to do to-day."

Lord Ticehurst left his Mentor, after shaking hands warmly with him, and took his departure in a very happy frame of mind. It was a great comfort to him to have made Lloyd aware of the state of his feelings towards Miss Lambert, immature as those feelings were, for Mentor had such a hold over the young man that he never felt comfortable while he was keeping anything back from him. But when he was gone, Gilbert Lloyd did not begin to write the letter to Windsor, or settle to any of the "heap of work" which he had mentioned as in store for him. He got up and opened a drawer full of cigars, selected one carefully, lit it, and threw himself into a low easy-chair, with his legs crossed, and his hands clasped behind his head. At first he puffed angrily at his cigar, but after a little time he gradually began to smoke more quietly, and then he unclasped his hands and rested his elbows on his knees, and his chin on his hands.

" That's it!" he said aloud, " that's the line of country! Fancy my never having given a thought to where this fellow was going so often, never wondering at the sudden fancy he had taken to his aunt's society; and then discovering from his own lips that he has been paying visits to my wife! More than that—that he is confoundedly in love with her, and wants to marry her! Wants to marry my wife! There's something deuced funny in that. I wonder whether any other fellow ever had a man come to him and tell him he wanted to marry his wife. I should think not! Not that I should care in the least if anyone married Gertrude—anyone, that is to say, except this youth downstairs. I have not done with him

yet, and a wife would interfere horribly with me
and my plans. Yes, that's the right notion. There
is no reason why Etchingham should not be encouraged in this new fancy. It will keep him
from dangling after any other woman, and it can
come to nothing. I know her ladyship of Carabas
rather too well to credit her with any desire for
Miss Lambert the opera-singer as a relative; as a
plaything, an amusement, she's well enough : but
Lady Carabas cries ' *Halte là !*' and a hint from
me to her would make her speak the word. Besides, *I* am not dead yet, and I might have something to say about my wife's second marriage—
that is, of course, supposing that second marriage
did not suit my views. But there will be no
question of that for some time. Now that I know
the state of affairs, I can keep myself *au courant* to
all that goes on through Lady Carabas; I shall
make her ladyship induce her charming nephew
to moderate his transports so far as any question
of proposing is concerned; but he may be ' awful
spoons,' as he charmingly phrases it, as long as he
pleases. As for this Windsor notion, that must be

knocked on the head at once. I don't intend to give up the Cup-day at Ascot myself, and I certainly could not well be there, if Gertrude were to be of the party. I'll settle that with Lady Carabas."

Here behold Gilbert Lloyd's philosophy and views of life. Affection for the woman whom he had wedded, and from whom he had separated, he had not one scrap ; nor even care as to what she did, what course of life she pursued, whence she obtained the means of livelihood. Any interest in that he had abnegated when he accepted the terms which she dictated for their separation,—terms which meant oblivion of the past and *insouciance* for the future, terms which he had indorsed when they were proposed, and which he was ready to hold to still. But when his knowledge of his wife's previous life—of the thrall from which she had actually, but not legally, escaped—gave him the mastery over her actions, or the actions of those in relation with her, he was prepared to twist the screw to its tightest, if by so twisting it he could aid in the development of his own plans.

Had Gilbert Lloyd no remnant of love for Gertrude, no lingering reminiscence of the time when, a trusting school-girl, she placed her future in his hands, gave up her whole life to him, and fled away from the only semblance of home which she had known at his suggestion? Had he no thought of the time immediately succeeding that, when for those few happy weeks, ere the pleasant dream was dispelled, she lay nestling in his bosom, building O such castles in the air, such impossible pictures, prompted by girlish romantic fancies of the future? Had Gilbert Lloyd any such reminiscences as these? Truth to tell, not in the smallest degree. He had passed the wet sponge over the slate containing any records of his early life, and all trace of Gertrude had been effectually erased. When he heard of her now, when it became necessary for him to give a certain number of moments to thinking of her in connection with business matters, he treated the affair simply from a business point of view. To him she was as dead "as nail in door," as immaterial as the first woman he might brush

against in the street; she might be turned to
serve certain ends which he had in view; but he
regarded her simply as one of the puppets in the
little life-drama of which he acted as showman.

The pleasant gathering which Lord Ticehurst
had looked forward to on the Cup-day at Ascot
did not come off. Gilbert Lloyd had five minutes'
interview with Lady Carabas on the subject;
and two days afterwards Mr. Boulderson Munns
announced the impossibility of his sparing Miss
Grace Lambert's services for that evening. Not
that Miss Lambert would have accepted Lord
Ticehurst's hospitality if her services could have
been spared, but it was best to put the refusal on
a strictly professional footing. Mr. Lloyd did not
in the least care about absenting himself from
that pleasant gathering on the Heath, and it was
of course impossible for him to be brought face to
face with Lord Ticehurst's intended guest. So
the recipients of his lordship's hospitality in the
cottage at Windsor were Lady Carabas and Miss
Macivor, a sprightly elderly spinster, who was as
well known in society as the clock at St. James's

Palace, and who was always ready to play what she imagined to be propriety in any fast party. The ladies enjoyed themselves immensely, they said; but their host's gratification was not so keen. He was bored and ruffled, and he did not care to disguise it.

And now a change came over Gilbert Lloyd, which was to him unaccountable, and against which he struggled with all the power of his strong will, but struggled in vain. This change came about, as frequently happens with such matters by which our whole future is influenced, in an unforeseen manner, and by the merest accident. The Ascot settling-day had not passed off very comfortably. Several heavy book-makers were absent; among them one who had lost a large sum of money to the Ticehurst party. This man was known to have won hugely on the Derby a fortnight before, and to have had a capital account at his banker's a few days previously. It seemed therefore clear to Gilbert Lloyd, with whom the management of the matter rested, that the money was still in the possession of the ab-

sconding book-maker, who would, in all probability, take an opportunity of leaving the country
with the sum thus accumulated. Gilbert Lloyd
put himself in communication with the police au-
thorities, furnished a correct description of the
defaulter, and caused a strict watch to be kept at
the various principal ports. One morning he received a telegram from Liverpool, announcing
that the offender had been seen there. It had
been ascertained that he was about to leave by
the Cunard boat for Boston the next morning;
but that, as he had committed no criminal offence,
it was impossible for the police to detain him.
This news made Gilbert Lloyd furious; that he
should have his prey under his hand, and yet be
unable to close that hand upon him, was maddening. He thought some good might be effected
by his hurrying to Liverpool by the afternoon
express, finding the defaulter, and frightening him
out of at least a portion of the money due. The
more he turned this plan in his mind, the more
feasible it seemed to him, and the more he was
determined to carry it into effect. There were,

however, certain affairs to be transacted that day upon which it was most necessary he should, before starting, communicate personally with Lord Ticehurst; and Gilbert, from recent experience, knew that he should have considerable difficulty in tracing that young nobleman's whereabouts. He made inquiries at all the various haunts, but without any success; at length, at the club someone said that Ticehurst had offered to drive him down to the Crystal Palace, for which place he had started a couple of hours ago. The Crystal Palace! What on earth could take him there? Gilbert Lloyd, who saw fewer "sights" than almost any man in London, had been there once, but brought away a dazed recollection of fountains and Egyptian idols, and statues and tropical trees, none of which he thought would have any interest for his pupil. But his wonderment was at an end when, taking up the newspaper and looking for the advertisement, he saw announced that a grand concert, by the principal singers of the Scandinavian Opera, would take place at the Crystal Palace that afternoon, and that the chief attraction of the concert was to be Miss Grace Lambert.

A swift hansom bore him to Victoria, and a tedious train landed him at the Crystal Palace, just in time to hear the opening notes of Herr Boreas' solo on the ophicleide. A charming performance that of Herr Boreas, but one to which Mr. Lloyd gave no attention. He hurried through the crowd, looking eagerly right and left; and at last his eyes fell upon a group, where they remained.

Lord Ticehurst, Mr. Munns, and two or three others were component parts of this little knot; but Gilbert Lloyd saw but one person—Gertrude. How marvellously she had improved during the time that had elapsed since they parted! She had been pretty as a girl; she was lovely as a woman. How lovely she looked in her simple morning dress and coquettish little bonnet! With what a perfect air of easy grace she listened to the men bending before her, and how quietly she received the homage which they were evidently paying! An angry flush rose on Gilbert's pale cheeks, and his heart beat quickly as he witnessed this manifest adoration. What right had anyone but he to approach her, to—It stung him like a cut from a whip, it flared like a train of gunpowder. He knew what it was in an instant: mad, raging, ungovernable jealousy—nothing else. He had thrown off all love for her—all thought of her; and now, the first time they met, the passion which struck him when he first saw her, years before, looking out of the window of the Vale House, sprung up with renewed fury within him, and he raged and chafed as he recognised the obstacles which kept him from her, but which were no barriers to other men. She seemed utterly indifferent to them, though, he was glad to see—no! her face lights up, she smiles and bends forward; and when she looks up again there is a blush upon her cheek. Who has been speaking to her?—the tall handsome man with the brown beard—Miles Challoner! And Gilbert Lloyd swore a deep oath of revenge —revenge of which his wife and his brother should each bear their share.

CHAPTER III.

To Herr Boreas was allotted the pleasing duty of opening the concert. The jolly German gentleman, neatly and seasonably dressed in black, with a large diamond-brooch in his plaited shirt-front, and with stuffy-looking black-cloth boots with shiny tips, opened his big chest, and puffed away at his ophicleide, evoking now the loudest and now the softest notes; while the crowds kept pouring in to the railed-off space, and took their seats, laughing and chattering, and not paying the smallest attention to the performance. It was a great day at the Palace, a day on which great people thought it proper to be seen there. The little public-houses in the neighbourhood were filled with resplendent creatures in gorgeous

liveries, whose employers were making their way
through nave and transept, looking at nothing
save the other people there, and looking at them
as though they were singular specimens of humanity specially put out for show. In the matter of
staring, it must be confessed that the other people
returned the compliment. The regular attendants
at the Crystal Palace are, for the most part, resi-
dent in the neighbourhood, and the neighbouring
residents are, for the most part, of or belonging
to the City. The brokers of stocks, shares, and
sugar; the owners of Manchester warehouses, the
riggers of markets, and the projectors of companies; the directors of banks, and the "floaters"
of "concerns," have, many of them, charming
villas, magnificent mansions, or delicious snug-
geries at Blackheath, Eltham, or Sydenham; and
the Palace is the great place of resort for their
wives and daughters, and for themselves when
the cares of business are laid aside. How many
successful matches, in which money has been
allied to money, have commenced in flirtations
by the side of the plashing fountains, or in the

shade of the stunted orange-trees! What execution has not been done by flashing eyes in the central promenade! There, by the Dying Gladiator, Lord Claude Votate proposed for Miss Meggifer, and secured the fortune which rescued the Calfington estates from his lordship's creditors; there, behind the Dancing Faun, Charles Partington, of Partington Nephews, kissed Minnie Black, daughter of Black Brothers—was seen to do it by Mrs. Black, consequently could not escape, and thus cemented an alliance between those hitherto rival houses, considered in Wood-street as the Horatii and Curiatii of the Berlin-wool trade. Pleasant place of decorous festivity and innocent diversion, whence instruction has been completely routed by amusement, and where the Assyrian gods and the Renaissance friezes are deserted for the dancing dogs and the Temple of Momus as constructed by Mr. Nelson Lee!

By the time that Herr Boreas had finished his solo—which was not until he had blown all the breath out of his body, and was apparently on the

verge of apoplexy—the audience had taken possession of all the seats; and as the German gentleman bowed himself out of the orchestra, amidst
a great deal of applause from people who, indeed,
could not help having heard, but had not paid the
least attention to him, there was a general reference to the programmes to see what was coming
next, then a rustling, a whispering, and that
curious settling stir which electrically runs through
an audience just before the advent of a favourite
artist.   Gilbert Lloyd, not insensible to this, involuntarily looked round from behind the pillar
by which he was standing to the spot where he
had seen Gertrude, but she was no longer there.
The next instant thunders of applause rang through
the building as she advanced upon the platform.
She bowed gracefully but coldly; then the conductor waved his baton, and dead silence fell upon
the audience, leaning forward with outstretched
necks to catch the first notes of her voice.   Soft
and sweet, clear and trilling, comes the bird-like
song, warbled without the smallest apparent effort,
while thrilling the listeners to the heart—thrilling

Gilbert Lloyd, who holds his breath, and looks on in rapture. He had heard her before, but in Italian opera; now she is singing an English ballad, of no great musical pretension indeed, but pretty and sympathetic. At the end of the first verse the applause burst out in peals on peals; and so carried away was Gilbert Lloyd, that he found himself joining in the general feeling—he who scarcely knew one note of music from another, and who had come to the place on a matter of important business. That must stand over now, though—he felt that. The absconding turfite might go to America, or to the deuce, for the matter of that; Gilbert Lloyd felt it an impossibility to leave the place where he then was, and tried to cheat himself by pretending that it was expedient for his own interest that he should keep a close watch upon Lord Ticehurst just at that time. That young nobleman certainly took no pains to conceal his warm admiration for Miss Lambert, and his intense delight at her performance. He applauded more loudly than anyone else, and assumed an attitude of rapt attention, which would have been highly interesting if it had not also been slightly comic. When the song ceased, the cries for a repetition were loud and universal. Gertrude, who had retired, again advanced to the front of the orchestra. By an involuntary impulse, Gilbert Lloyd stepped from behind the pillar which had hitherto shielded him, and their eyes met—met for the first time since he left her at the Brighton hotel, on the day of Harvey Gore's death.

A deep flush overspread Gilbert Lloyd's usually pallid cheeks, but Gertrude's expression did not change in the slightest degree. Not a trace of the faintest emotion, even of curiosity, could be seen in her face. The conductor of the orchestra, just before he left her in front of the audience, addressed some remark to her; and as she replied, Gilbert noticed that her lips were curling with a slight sneer—an expression which he fancied he understood, when the band commenced to play an air which even he, all unmusical as he was, recognised as "Home, sweet home." But she never looked at him again during the

song, which she sung even more sweetly than the
first, and with a deep pathos that roused the
audience to enthusiasm. Gilbert Lloyd kept his
eyes fixed on her, never moving them for an
instant; and as he marked the calm air with
which she received the public applause, and the
graceful ease of all her movements—as he saw
how her face, always clear cut and classically
moulded, had ripened in womanly beauty and
intellectual expression—as he noticed the rounded
elegance of her figure, the tasteful simplicity of
her dress—and he noticed all these details down
to the fit of her gloves and the colour of her
bonnet-strings—he raged against himself for having been fool enough to relinquish the hold he
once had on her. Could that hold be reëstab-
lished? If he were again to have an opportunity
—But while these thoughts were passing through
his mind, Gertrude had finished her song and
quitted the orchestra, and her glance had not
fallen on him again.

Meantime Gilbert Lloyd saw he had been
noticed by the group with whom Miss Lambert

had been sitting previous to her performance, and
as Miles Challoner was no longer with them he
thought it better to join the party. His appearance amongst them was evidently a surprise to
Lord Ticehurst, who expressed the greatest astonishment at his Mentor's finding any amusement in so slow a proceeding as a concert, and
who grew very red and looked very conscious
when Gilbert asked him what particular charm
such an entertainment could possess for him.
Lord Sandilands was, as usual in his behaviour
to Mr. Lloyd, scrupulously polite, but not particularly cordial. He had nothing in common
with Gilbert, detested the turf and all its associations, and looked on Lord Ticehurst's turf
Mentor as very little better than Lord Ticehurst's
stud-groom. Mr. Boulderson Munns still remained with them, and intended so to remain.
It was part of Mr. Munns' business that he
should be seen in close and confidential communication " with two nobs," as he elegantly phrased
it, and he took advantage of the opportunity.
Nothing pleased him so much as to notice when

members of the promenading crowd would elbow each other, look towards him, and whisper together, or when he saw heads bent forward and opera-glasses pointed in his direction. It was his concert, he thought: when Herr Boreas blew his ophicleide, or Miss Lambert sang her song, he felt inclined to place his thumbs in the arm-holes of his big white waistcoat, and go forward and acknowledge the applause. He had done so in former years in the transformation-scenes of pantomimes, when the people called for Scumble the scene-painter, and why not now? Boreas and the Lambert were quite as much his people as Scumble! Mr. Munns restrained himself, however, from motives of policy. It was pretty plain to him, as he afterwards explained to Mr. Duff, that this young swell, this Ticehurst, was dead spoons on the Lambert; and as he had no end of money, and was good for a box every night, and perhaps something more if the screw were properly put on, it would be best to make it all sugar for 'em. With this laudable intent he commenced talking loudly to Lord Ticehurst of Miss Lambert's attractions, and did not suffer himself to be interrupted for more than a minute by Lloyd's arrival.

"As I was telling you, my lord," he recommenced, "she's a wonder, this—this young lady—a wonder, and nothing but it! Not merely for the hit she's made, though it's a great go, and I don't mean to deny it; but I don't go by the public, I know too much of them. Why, Lord Sandilands here, he remembers when—Well, it's no good going into that; lots of them we've seen in our time, and then, after a season or two, all dickey! regular frost! But there's something very different from that with Miss Lambert—so quiet, and so quite the lady; none of your flaring up, and ballyragging the people about. Why Miss Murch, our wardrobe-woman, said to me only last night, that she only wished the other prima donnas were like her—won't wear this, and won't wear that—How d'ye do, Mr. Lloyd? I was talking to his lordship of Miss Lambert, who's just been singing, and saying what a stunner she was. Now, if you've got a filly to name—one that's likely to be something, and do something, you · know—you should call her Grace Lambert—"

"No, I think not; not quite that, Mr. Munns!" interposed Lord Ticehurst; "that's scarcely the kind of compliment I should care to pay to Miss Lambert."

"You may depend upon it that it's one which, if Miss Lambert had the option, she would scarcely care to accept, my lord," said Lord Sandilands tartly; "however, there she is to answer for herself;" and he pointed through the glass to the garden, where Gertrude was seen walking with Mrs. Bloxam. There was an evident intention on the part of all composing the group to join them, and seeing this Gilbert Lloyd would have withdrawn; but Lord Ticehurst took him by the arm, and saying, "I've long wanted to introduce you to Miss Lambert, old fellow, and now you can't possibly escape," led the way.

If he were ever again to have an opportunity! Had that opportunity then come? Was his never-failing luck holding by him still, and giving him this chance of retrieving the blunder he had made in the Brighton hotel? He thought so. His breath came short and thick as he nerved himself for the meeting. He saw her as she and Mrs. Bloxam strolled before them up the garden-walk, noticed the swimming ease of her gait, the fall of her black-lace cloak, as it hung from her shoulders, the graceful pose of her head. She turned, he heard the sound of her approaching feet, he felt her presence close opposite to him, he heard Lord Ticehurst's voice repeating the set formula of introduction, but he saw nothing until he looked up to catch the faintest inclination of Gertrude's head, and to see her face colder, more set, more rigid than ever. Neither spoke; and the silence was becoming awkward, when Lord Ticehurst said, "I imagine you must have heard me speak of my friend Lloyd, Miss Lambert? Good enough to manage my racing matters for me, and to manage them deuced well—with the greatest talent and skill, and all that kind of thing. Not in your line, I know, Miss Lambert; but still—still—" and his lordship's eloquence failed him, and he broke down.

Again neither of them spoke, but Gilbert Lloyd looked up from under his brow, and saw the stony glance which Gertrude cast upon him for an instant, then turned to Mrs. Bloxam, and suggested that they should return to the concert-room, where she would speedily be wanted. Lord Sandilands was at her right hand, Lord Ticehurst on the other side of Mrs. Bloxam. Mr. Munns preceded them, and caused a great sensation, on which he had reckoned, when he flung open the door and ostentatiously ushered them into the building; but Gilbert Lloyd walked slowly behind, his hands plunged into his pockets, and his face—there was no one to heed him, no reason for him to don an unnatural expression—savage, set, and careworn.

So it had come at last, he thought. They had met after so long an estrangement; and that was to be the end of the meeting. No recognition— he had not expected that—no public recognition, no hint that they had ever been anything to each other. He recollected the words that he had addressed to her on their parting; they came surging up and ringing in his ears: "It is not very likely that we shall ever run across each other's path in the future, but if we do, we meet as entire strangers; and the fact of our having been anything to one another must never be brought forward to prejudice any scheme in which either of us may be engaged." Memory brought before him the dingy cold room of the second-rate hotel, with the dying sunlight streaking its discoloured walls, in which these words had been spoken; brought before him the slight figure and the deadly pallid face of the girl as she listened to them, and acquiesced in their verdict. In that verdict she acquiesced still, was acting up to its spirit, to its very letter. It was his proposition to leave her alone and unfettered " in any scheme in which she might be engaged." The fooling, the enslavement of this idiot Ticehurst, who was a mere tool in his hands, was the game which she was now playing, at which he was to look on helplessly, having himself spoken the words which rendered her independent of his control.

And she, how did she take it? Calmly enough; but not so calmly as Gilbert Lloyd supposed. She had never gone in for much feeling, and whatever

she had was now completely at her command, far
more completely even than when she last had
parted from her husband. Moreover, while Gilbert had utterly given himself up to the business
of his turf profession, resolutely refusing to think
of his wife, or to acknowledge to himself that there
was ever a possibility of their again being brought
into contact, the chance of such a meeting had
often occurred to Gertrude, and the manner in
which she would demean herself, should the occasion arise, had been thought over by her and
settled in her mind. And now that it had arisen,
so far as her outward demeanour was concerned,
she had behaved herself exactly as she had always
proposed. And her facial control was such, that
no one looking at her could have an inkling of
what was passing in her mind, which was fortunate on this occasion, for she was considerably
more disturbed than she had expected. The first
sight of her husband was a complete shock to her,
and it was only by the exercise of the greatest
presence of mind that she prevented herself from
betraying her perturbation. When the first shock

was past—and she owed it to the strict discipline
of professional training that she was enabled to
get over it so quickly—her thoughts reverted to
the subject, and she was able to discuss it calmly
with herself.   What brought Gilbert Lloyd to
that place?   She knew him well enough to feel
sure that there must have been some strong in-
ducement, and what could that be?   Gilbert was
lié with Lord Ticehurst; and that that full-flavoured young nobleman was considerably in love
with her, Gertrude had never attempted to disguise from herself; but what could that matter
to the man from whom she had been so long
estranged, and who had never shown the smallest
interest in her proceedings during that long estrangement?   The possibility of a desire on Gilbert's part to negotiate for a renewal of intimacy
crossed her mind for an instant, but was at once
rejected; and not even for an instant did she
imagine the desire for such a proceeding was
based on anything but motives of policy.   And,
after all, what did it matter to her?   To her
Gilbert Lloyd was dead and buried, she had

nothing to look for at his hands, nothing to fear from him—her lip curled as she recollected that; she would dismiss him entirely from her thoughts, she would—what could have brought him to that concert, of all places in the world? It might be useful to know something of his mode of life. She would lead Lady Carabas to talk of him; the marchioness would be only too happy to dilate on such a subject.

By the time Miss Lambert was to sing again, she had quite made up her mind on this point, and the sight of Gilbert Lloyd, *planté là*, did not cause her the slightest emotion. He stood as one rapt, fascinated by her beauty, drinking-in her voice, with one constant idea beating in his brain:— Was the past irrevocable? could not the mischief be undone? The power he had had in the old days remained to him still; he had but to exercise it, and all would be right again. True that just then she had rebuffed him; but that was her way, always had been; she had always piqued herself upon her pride, and after that had had its fling he should be able to do with her as he liked.

Miss Lambert was in full song as these thoughts passed through Gilbert Lloyd's mind, when suddenly she changed colour, a transient flush overspread her face, dying away again almost instantaneously. At the same instant, Gilbert Lloyd turned swiftly round in the direction in which he had noticed her glance fall, and saw Miles Challoner, who had recently entered and dropped into a chair just behind Lord Sandilands' seat. No doubt of it, no doubt of it; her self-command was so shaken that her voice faltered for an instant, and he—look at his eyes, fastened on her face with a look of perfect love and trust, and it was impossible to doubt the position. Lloyd's heart sunk within him at the sight, and a bitter oath was rising to his lips, and would have found utterance, when he felt his arm pressed, and looking round, saw Tommy Toshington, of the clubs, standing behind him. Mr. Toshington had on a new and curly wig, a light high muslin cravat, and looked bland and amiable. He winked affably at Lloyd, and laying his finger lightly against his nose, said, "You're wrong, my dear boy;—it's all right!" Mr. Gilbert Lloyd shortly bade his friend not to be an ass, but if he had anything to say, to out with it. Nothing abashed at the strength of Gilbert's language, Tommy said,

"My dear fellow, I mean exactly what I say; you're under a mistake, while all the time it's all right for *you!*"

"What's all right for me?—with whom?—where?"

"There!" said Tommy Toshington, wagging his new wig and his curly-brimmed hat in the direction where Lord Ticehurst was sitting; "his lordship is *entêté* with a certain warbler, eh? Fourth finger of the left hand—death do us part, and all that sort of thing, eh? That wouldn't suit your book, I should think—have to give up your rooms; she persuade him to cut the turf, go to church, and that kind of thing. Don't you be afraid, my boy; I know the world better than you, and that'll never come off!"

"You think not?" asked Gilbert.

"I'm sure not," replied Tommy. "Look here; he'd like it fast enough. Etchingham would marry her to-morrow if he got the chance; but she's full of pluck and spirit, and don't care a bit for him. How do I know? Because she cares for somebody else. How do I know that? My dear fellow, don't I know everything? What used the old Dook to say, 'Ask Toshington, he'll know; he knows everything, Tommy does.' And he didn't make many mistakes, the old Dook."

"Perhaps you know who is the 'somebody' else for whom the lady cares?" said Gilbert, an evil light dawning in his face, and his lips involuntarily tightening as he put the question.

"Of *course* I do!" said Tommy, with a crisp little laugh; "keep my eyes open, see everything; seen 'em together lots of times—Carabas House, Lady Lowndes', and lots of places. You know him, I should think; tall man from Gloucestershire—big beard—Chaldecott—some name like that!"

This time the oath broke from Lloyd's lips unchecked. He turned rapidly on his heel, and strode away.

"Dev'lish ill-bred young man that," said old Toshington, looking after him; "dammy, there's no manners left in the men of the present day!"

CHAPTER IV.

PURSUIT.

THE clearance effected under the superintend-
ence of the Office of Works, for the amalgama-
tion under one roof of the various Courts of
Law, has carried away a large portion of Cle-
ment's Inn, and has obliterated the pillared
entrance to that dusky but genial home of the
shady and impecunious. In the days of our
story, however, Inn and entrance were still
there; the former tenanted by human sheep of
various degrees of blackness—roistering govern-
ment-office clerks, with the Insolvent Court—
which at the outset of their career had been but
a light cloud as small as a man's hand, but
which year by year had assumed larger and
more definite proportions — ever lowering over
them; third-rate attorneys, who combined law

with discount, "doing" little bills for ten and
twenty pounds with the aforenamed government
clerks, and carefully putting in an appearance
at Somerset House on pay-days to receive their
money, or the refresher which was to induce the
withholding of the document — it is always "a
document"—until another quarter had elapsed;
agents for companies of all kinds of limited and
unlimited liability; newspaper writers obliged to
have cheap chambers in the neighbourhood of
their offices; foreigners representing continental
firms, and wanting a cheap and quasi-respectable
address; an actor or two, a score of needy men-
about-town, and a few Jews. Round the pillars
seethed and bubbled a scum of humanity of the
nastiest kind—vendors of the fried fish and the
pickled whelk, boot-blackers of abnormally horrid
appearance: and emaciated children from the
neighbouring Clare Market and the adjoining
courts, thieves and impostors from their infancy,
hung about the cab-rank, and added to the
general filth and squalor. A pleasant Slough
of Despond, that little spot, now standing bare

and cleared, surrounded by the balmy Holywell, the virtuous Wych, with Drury Lane running from it at right-angles, and the dirtiest corner of the great legal cobweb of courts and alleys at its back.

It was a hot morning in July when a cab drew up at the pillars, and Gilbert Lloyd jumped out, paid the driver, and made his way into the Inn. The exhalations from the barrows of the fried-fish vendors were potent, and the change to the faint, sickly perfume of the West-Indian pine-apple, tastefully arranged in slices on an open barrow which blocked the immediate thoroughfare, was scarcely refreshing. Perhaps in July the second-hand garments, even the uniforms, which the Jewish gentlemen who deal in such trophies hang up at the entrances of their warehouses, are a thought stronger in flavour than in the winter; and a fifth-hand portmanteau, which has seen a great deal of service under various owners, is apt, under the influence of the sun, to suggest its presence. But Gilbert Lloyd paid no heed to anything of this kind;

he had roughed it too long to care for what came between the wind and his nobility; not being a literary photographer on the look-out for "character," he paid no attention to any of the surroundings, but went straight on, making his way through the jostling crowd until he arrived at a door, on the posts of which was painted "Gammidge's Private-Inquiry Office, ground-floor." A further reference to the right-hand door of the first-floor discovered a still more elaborate placard, announcing that "Nichs. Gammidge, many years in the detective police, undertook inquiries of a private and confidential nature; agents all over the Continent; strictest secrecy observed; divorce cases particularly attended to; ring right-hand bell; and no connection with foreign impostors trading on N. G.'s new invention."

Gilbert Lloyd with some difficulty — for in the dingy passage there was but little light even on that bright summer morning — read this description, and in obedience to its suggestion pulled the right-hand bell. The sound of the

bell, vibrating loudly, apparently had the effect
of putting a sudden stop to a muttered conversation of a groaning character, which had been
dimly audible; the door was opened by a spring
from the inside, and Gilbert entered. He found
himself in a low-ceilinged dirty room, with no
other furniture than a couple of chairs and a
very rickety deal table. The windows were
covered more than half-way up with blinds
improvised out of old newspapers; a clock with
one hand was on the wall; an almanac, much
ink-scored and pin-marked, stood on the mantel-
shelf; and a limp map of Great Britain, evidently
torn out of an ancient *Bradshaw*, was pinned
behind the door. At first, on entering, Gilbert
Lloyd thought himself the sole occupant of the
room; but when his eyes had become accustomed
to the partial darkness, he discovered someone
rubbing himself against the wall at the opposite
end of the room, and apparently trying to squeeze
himself through into the next house. A little
hard looking at and careful study made him out
a very thin, small, white-faced young man, with

hollow cheeks, a sharp face, and a keen restless eye. As Gilbert's glance fell on him, or rather, as he seemed to feel it fall on him, he shook himself with an odd restless motion, as though to endeavour to get rid of some spell of fascination, but evidently desired to keep as much as possible in the background. The groaning, smothered conversation meanwhile had recommenced in another quarter, and Gilbert, looking round, noticed a door evidently leading into an inner room.

"Is this Mr. Gammidge's office?" he asked abruptly of the white-faced young man.

The white-faced young man gave a sudden start, as though a pin had been run into him, but never spoke.

"Mr. Gammidge's office—is this Mr. Gammidge's office?" repeated Gilbert.

"I—I believe so," said the white-faced young man, taken aback by the sharpness of the key in which the inquiry was made. "I have no reason to think it's not."

"Where is Mr. Gammidge?"

"Not in!" Wonderfully sharp and pert came this reply; constant lying in one groove oils the tongue so splendidly.

"Not in?" echoed Gilbert half savagely.

"Not in! Sure to be in later in the day. Got most important business on just now for—"

"Stow it!" The words came not from the white-faced young man, nor from Gilbert, but yet they were perfectly audible.

On hearing them, the white-faced young man became silent at once, and Gilbert looked round in amazement. The muttered groans became fainter, a sound as of clinking money was heard, then as of the opening of a door, the farewell of a gruff voice, the departure of a thick pair of boots; then one door slammed, and the inner door, which Gilbert had noticed on his first entrance, opened, and a man stood in the doorway with a beckoning forefinger.

A short stout man in a brown wig, with a fat unintelligent face, with heavy pendulous cheeks and a great jowl, and a round stupid chin, but with an eye like a beryl—small, bright, and luminous; a man with just sufficient intelligence to know that he was considerably overrated, and that the best chance for him in keeping up the deception lay in affectation of deepest mystery, and in saying as little as possible. Mr. Gammidge had been made a hero in certain police-cases during his professional career, by two or three " gentlemen of the press," who had described a few of his peculiarities—a peculiar roll of his head, a sonorous manner of taking snuff, a half-crow of triumph in his throat when he thought he saw his way out of a complication—in their various organs. Henceforth these peculiarities were his stock-in-trade, and he relied upon them for all his great personal effects.

When Gilbert Lloyd obeyed the influence of the beckoning forefinger, he passed through the door of communication between the inner and outer rooms, and found himself in an apartment smaller and not less dingy than that he had left. In the middle of it was a large desk, on which were a huge leaden inkstand, a few worn quill-pens, and a very inky blotting-pad. Sentinel on one flank stood a big swollen Post-office Directory, two years old; sentinel on the other, a stumpy manuscript volume in a loose binding, labelled "Cases." The walls blossomed with bills offering large sums as rewards for information to be given respecting persons who had absconded; and on a disused and paralytic green-cloth screen, standing in a helpless attitude close by the desk, was pinned a bill, setting forth the Sessions of the Central Criminal Court for the year, with the dates on which Mr. Gammidge was engaged in any of the trials pending distinguished by a broad cross with a black-lead pencil.

As soon as Gilbert Lloyd had entered the room, Mr. Gammidge closed the door carefully behind him, and placing himself in front of him, indulged him with the peculiar roll of the head, while he took a sonorous pinch of snuff, and said in a thick confidential voice, "Now, captin?"

"I'm no captain," said Lloyd shortly, "and you don't recollect me; though you're ready to swear you do, and though I have employed you before this."

Lloyd paused here for a moment; but as Mr. Gammidge merely looked at him helplessly, and muttered under his breath something about "such a many gents," he went on.

"My name is Gilbert Lloyd. I manage Lord Ticehurst's racing matters for him; and last year I employed you to look after one of our boys, who we thought was going wrong; do you recollect now?"

"Perfectly," said Mr. Gammidge, brightening. "Boy had been laid hold of by a tout from a sporting-paper, who was practisin' on him through his father, given to drink, and his sister, on 'oom the tout was supposed to be sweet."

"Exactly; well, you found that out clearly enough, and got us all the information required. Now I want you again."

"More boys goin' wrong, sir?" asked Mr. Gammidge. "They're the out-and-outest young scamps; they're that precocious and knowin'—"

"It's not a boy that I want to know about this time," said Lloyd, checking the flow of his companion's eloquence; "it's a woman."

"That's more in my way; three-fourths of my business is connected with them. Did you 'appen to take any notice of the young man in that room as you came through? He's the best 'nose' in London. Find out anything. Lor' bless you, that young man have been in more divorce cases then the Serjeant himself. He can hide behind a walking-stick, and see through the pipe of a Chubb's latch-key. There's nothing like him in London."

"Put him on to my business at once, then. Look at this card." Mr. Gammidge produced a large pair of tortoiseshell-rimmed double eye-glasses, and proceeded to make an elaborate investigation. "You know the name? I thought so. Now, your man must keep account of everyone who goes in here by day or night, so long as she's at home; and when she goes out he must follow her, and, so far as he can, find out who speaks to her, and where. There is a five-pound note to begin with. You understand?"

"You may look upon it as good as done, sir," said Mr. Gammidge, commencing to make a mem-

orandum of the number and date of the bank-note
in his pocket-book, "and to let you know at the
old address?"

"No; when he has anything to tell, drop me
a line, and I'll meet him here. Good-day."

The white-faced young man, entering fully
into his new occupation, speedily deserved the
encomiastic remarks which had been lavished upon
him by his principal, and in a short time Mr.
Lloyd was furnished with full information as to
the personal appearance of the various visitors at
the Bayswater villa, and of the friends whom Miss
Lambert was in the habit of meeting away from
her home. In both these categories Gilbert Lloyd
found, as he had expected to find, a very accurate
representation of Miles Challoner. The information, all expected as it was, irritated and chafed
him; and he gave up a whole day to considering
how he could best put a stop to the ripening intimacy between Miles and Gertrude, or, at all
events, weaken it. Finally, he decided on paying
a visit to Mrs. Bloxam, and seeing whether she
could not be frightened with a suspicion, perfectly

undefined, of something horrible and mysterious
which would take place if the intimacy were permitted to go on unchecked. Accordingly, upon
a day when the white-faced young man had ascertained that Miss Lambert would be for some time
absent from home, Mr. Lloyd presented himself
at the Bayswater villa, and, without sending in
his name, followed the servant into the room,
where Mrs. Bloxam was seated. At first sight of
the man who had dared in former days to invade
the sanctity of her sheepfold and carry off one of
her pet lambs, the old lady was exceedingly indig-
nant, and her first impulse was to order the in-
truder to leave the house; but a moment's reflection convinced her that as he yet had the
power of being exceedingly dangerous to Gertrude,
or, at all events, of causing her the greatest
annoyance, it would be better to temporise. She
therefore listened to all Gilbert Lloyd's bland
assurances that, although there was an unfortunate
estrangement between his wife and himself, he
took the greatest interest in her career, and it was
purely as a matter of friendship that he had come

to warn her, through her ablest and best friend, of the danger she incurred in forming a certain acquaintance. So well did Mrs. Bloxam play her listening part, and so earnest was she in her thanks to her informant, that even the *rusé* turfite was taken in, and went away convinced that he had made his *coup*.

A few days afterwards he called again, and this time asked for Miss Lambert. The servant said that Miss Lambert was out. For Mrs. Bloxam: Mrs. Bloxam was out. Gilbert Lloyd then took out a card and handed it to the servant, begging her to give it to her mistress; but the servant, just glancing at it, handed it back, saying she had strict orders, in case the gentleman bearing that name ever called again, to refuse him admittance, and to return his card.

CHAPTER V.

REBUFFED.

THE cool determination of Gertrude's conduct, the resolution which did not shrink from a proceeding calculated to excite at least observation by her servants, took Gilbert Lloyd completely by surprise. Concealing, by a desperate effort, the passion of anger which flamed up in him, he turned away from the door, and got into the hansom awaiting him; but when quite out of sight of the gilded-bronze gates, and the miniature plantation of the Bayswater villa, he stopped the cab, got out, and pulling his hat down over his brow, walked on rapidly, in a mood strange indeed to his calculating and self-contained nature.

By what fatality had this woman once more turned up in his life—this woman of whom he was well rid, his marriage with whom had been a mistake—a failure—and his parting with whom had been the commencement of a new and decidedly fortunate era in his life? His thoughts were in a whirl, and for a time resisted his attempts to reduce them to order and sequence. The physical convulsion of rage claimed to have its way first, and had it. He had known that feeling many times in his life—the maddening anger which turns the face white and the lips livid, which makes the heart beat with suffocating throbs, and dims the sight. He knew all about that, and he had to bear it now, and to bear it in silence, without the relief of speech, with only the aid of solitude. He could not swear at Gertrude now, as he had done many a time when annoyance had come to him through her; he could not insult, threaten, strike her now; and much of the fury he felt was due to the powerlessness which drove him nearly mad, and which was his own doing. Ay, that was the worst of it, the least endurable part of the wrath which raged within him. This woman, who had been in his power, and had been made to experience the full significance of her

position; who had loved him once, and of whom
he had wearied, as it was in his nature to weary
of any desired object when attained,—this woman
held him in supreme indifference and contempt,
and set him at naught without fear or hesitation.
In the force and irrationality of his anger, he
forgot that she was acting quite within the letter
and the spirit of the convention made between
them; that he it was who had abandoned its
spirit at almost the first sight of her, and had
now received a humiliating check in endeavouring
to violate its letter. For a long time his anger
was blind, fierce, and unreasoning—directed almost
as much against himself as against Gertrude—
his wife! his wife! as he called her a hundred
times over, in the vain assertion of a position
which he had voluntarily abdicated, and which he
knew, in the bottom of his angry heart—even
while the anger seethed within it—he would not
be prepared to resume, were the opportunity
afforded him. But as he walked on and on, getting by degrees into outlying regions of the far
west—almost as little known to him as Cali-

fornia—the habit of calculation, of arranging his thoughts, of (metaphorically) laying his head on the exact process or combination which he required—a faculty and habit of which he felt the value every day—resumed its sway over him, and he no longer raged blindly about what had happened, but set himself to think it out. This, then, was a *parti pris* on the part of Gertrude; this, then, was a game in which he was her adversary —with a purpose to gain; she—his, with nothing in view but his defeat. Her cards were resolute ignoring of his existence; the absolute and inexorable adherence to the agreement made between them at Brighton. His cards were persistent following and watching of her, which the coincidences of his position and the facility with which he could make her circle of acquaintance his, added to the exigencies of her professional career, which she could not control, however unwelcome they might be, rendered easy of playing. The next question was, what end did he propose to himself in this sudden revulsion of feeling, this sudden irruption into his prosperous and pleasant life of an element which he had hoped, intended, and believed to be banished from it for ever? This question he could not answer clearly. The mists of anger and jealousy arose between him and the outline of his purpose. Was it to undo the past? Was it to woo and win once more this woman, whom he had driven away from him, and who had just made evident to him the weakness of his determination and the strength of her own? Was it to put himself entirely and unreservedly under the yoke of her power, from whose possible imposition he had been glad to escape by the final expedient to which he had resorted? Had he any such rash, insane notion as this in his thoughts? He did not know, he was not certain; he was not sure of anything but this—that Gertrude had refused to see him, and that he was resolved she should, come what might; she should not carry that point, she should not have the triumph at once of fidelity to their strange unnatural compact on her own part, and of having forced him to break it on his. He had dismissed her easily enough from his thoughts, but he could not dis-

miss her from them now; she kept possession of
them now, in the pride of her beauty—how handsome she was! he had never supposed she would
have grown into such commanding, self-possessed
beauty as hers was now—and in the triumph of
her talent—as she had never done since the brief
earliest days of their disastrous marriage. Gilbert
Lloyd was a man on whom success of any kind
produced a strong impression. It counted for
much in the rekindling of his former passion for
Gertrude that she was now a successful artist, her
supposed name in everyone's mouth, holding her
own before the world, a woman with a position,
an *entourage*, and an independent career. His
thoughts wandered away among scenes which he
had long forgotten, in which she was the central
figure, and into imaginary pictures of her present
life; and he repeated over and over again, with
rage—waxing dull by this time—" But she is my
wife! she is my wife! no matter what she chooses
to do, no matter how she chooses to act towards
me, she is my wife! I have only to declare it if I
choose." And the consequences to which she,

judging by her present conduct, would probably be entirely indifferent—was he prepared to face them? He could not answer this question either; he was not yet cool-headed enough to estimate them aright.

A devouring curiosity concerning Gertrude took possession of him—a craving eagerness to know what were her movements, who were her associates, how she lived; even the disposition of the rooms in her house, and her domestic relations. The absolute ignorance of all these things in which he remained, though his imperious will demanded to be informed of them, exasperated him; and with his fruitless anger there was mingled a grim humour, as he thought of the scenes through which they had passed together, as he recalled Gertrude in the intimacy of their domestic life. And now he was the one person in the world from whom she concealed herself, the one person shut out from her by a barrier erected by her inflexible will. Was he? Time would tell. He had not been ignorant during the sometimes stormy, sometimes gay and careless, but always unsatisfactory, period which preceded their separation, that he was by no means so indifferent to Gertrude as she was to him. On the contrary, he had realised that clearly and plainly, and it had sharpened his anger towards her and hardened his heart in the hour of their parting; and he had hated her then, and chafed under the knowledge that she did not hate him, that she was only glad to be rid of him, had only ceased utterly to love him, and learned utterly to despise him. Justly esteeming himself to be a good hater, Gilbert Lloyd found it difficult to understand how it was that he had so soon ceased to hate Gertrude, had so easily yielded to the sense of relief in having done with all that portion of his life in which she had a share, and had never had any serious thought of her, or speculation about her future; for to such an extent had his cynicism gone now that this period of oblivion and ease had in its turn expired, and she had again crossed his path to trouble him. He could only account for this curious phase through which he had passed by what seemed to him an insufficient reason—the new interests in his life, the success which attended his speculation in that "rich brute Ticehurst's" affairs—for thus did the more fastidious and not less vicious man of the two characterise, in his meditations, the coarse animal he was devoting himself so successfully to *exploiter*. Such a chance, after so long a run of ill-luck, varied only by a *coup* on which he preferred not to dwell in remembrance—a chance, as he thought, with an ominous darkening of his evil face, which, if it had only been afforded him a little sooner, might have averted the necessity for such a *coup*, was calculated to occupy him entirely, and banish from his mind anything which might divert him from the pursuit of his object.

And now it seemed wonderful to him that he could have thus forgotten her—now, when he was under the renewed spell of her beauty and her scorn.

There was an extraordinary fascination for him, even in the midst of his anger, in the mingled strangeness and familiarity with which she presented herself to his mind. He had a good deal of imagination, though but little poetry, in his nature, and the extraordinarily exceptional position of this woman and himself—the strangeness of the knowledge that she had accepted the fact of there being nothing mutual or even relative in their position now or ever—appealed, in the midst of his passion, to his imagination.

That she should dare to treat him thus,—that she should know him so little as to dare to treat him thus. He thought this, he said this more than once through his shut teeth; but he was not a fool, even in his rage, and he knew he was talking folly to himself in the moment that he uttered the words. Why should she not dare? Indeed, there was no daring about it. He had made the position for himself, and he was for the first time brought face to face with all the details of it. What was that position externally in the world's sight, in the only point of view in which he had any practical right to consider it? Just this: Miss Lambert did not choose to admit him to her acquaintance. He was helpless; she was in her right. He might force her to meet him in

the houses of other people—at the Marchioness of
Carabas' house, for instance—simply because she
could not afford, out of consideration for her own
social position, to give up her patroness; and also
(he began to understand Gertrude now sufficiently
to know that this second argument was by far the
stronger), because she would never suffer the consideration of meeting or not meeting him to influence her actions, to form a motive of her conduct in the smallest degree. He felt that with a
smart twinge of pain, the keen pain of mortified
self-love. He had simply ceased to exist for her
—that was all; she had taken the full sense of
their convention, and was acting on it *tout bonne-
ment.* He might, therefore, calculate safely upon
meeting her, without her consent, at other houses
than her own; but, forcing or inducing her to
admit him there, was, he felt, entirely beyond his
power. He was wholly insensible to the extreme
incongruity of such a possibility, had it existed;
and no wonder, for in their position all was incon-
gruous, and propriety or impropriety had lost their
meaning.

In the conflict of feeling and passion in which Gilbert Lloyd was thus engaged, there was no element of fierce contention wanting. Love, or the debased feeling which he called and believed to be love, and which fluctuated between passion and hate, baffled design, undefined fear, and jealousy, in which not merely Gertrude was concerned, but another who had a place in his life of still darker and more fatal meaning, and a more bitterly resented influence over his fate. When he had fought out the skirmish with the newly reawakened love for the wife whom he had almost forgotten, and been beaten, and had been forced to surrender so much of the disputed ground to the enemy, fear marshalled its forces against him, and pressed him hard. But not to the point of victory. Gilbert Lloyd was a man with whom fear had never had much chance; and if he had yielded somewhat to its influence in the separation from his wife, it was because that influence had been largely supported by long-smouldering discontent, *ennui*, a coincidence of convenience and opportunity, and a deserved conviction that the full potency of Gertrude's will was at work in the matter. There was little likelihood that fear should master him now; but it was there, and he had to stand, and repel its assaults. If he attempted to molest, to control Gertrude in any way; if it even became her interest or her pleasure to get rid of him in actual fact, in addition to their convenient theory,—fear asked him, Can she not do so? Is she not mistress of the situation, of every point of it? And he answered, Yes. If she chose to carry out the divorce—which they had mutually instituted without impertinent legal interference—would he dare to intervene? He remembered how he had speculated upon the expediency of encouraging the "rich brute's" *penchant* for the fashionable singer, when he had no suspicion who the fashionable singer was; and a rush of fury surged all over him as he thought, if she had chosen to encourage him, to marry him, for his rank, would he, Gilbert Lloyd, her husband, have dared to interfere? Fear had the best of it there; but he would not be beaten by fear.

This enemy was strong mainly because he could not rightly calculate its strength. How much did Gertrude know, or how little? Was it knowledge, or suspicion only, which had prompted her to the decision she had adopted, and the prompt action she had taken upon it? To these questions it was impossible he could get any answer; and he would, or thought he would, just then —for he was an unlikely man to stick to such a bargain, if he could have made it—have given years of his life to know what had passed that memorable day at Brighton, before he had returned to the death-bed of his friend, and there encountered Gertrude. The dying whisper which had conveyed to the young woman the power she had used so promptly was unknown by Lloyd; on this point—the great, the essential point of his musings—all was conjecture, dark, terrifying, and undefined.

Had love and fear only possessed his dark soul between them, the strife might soon have ended, in a division in which the man's own safety would have been consulted. Gilbert Lloyd

would have made up his mind that, as his first
fancy for Gertrude had passed away, so this
eccentric renewal of it would also harmlessly
decline. The whole difficulty might have resolved itself into his persuading Ticehurst to go
abroad in his company, until the "rich brute"
should have escaped all risk of an "entanglement,"
which Lloyd would have painted in the most
alarming colours, and Lloyd himself have recovered from a passing fit of weak folly, which
he might have been trusted to learn to despise,
on a sober consideration of its bearing on his
interests in the career in which he had contrived with so much difficulty to *lancer* himself.

But the look which he had seen in Gertrude's
proud calm face—the smile which was so absolutely new to him, that it would have thrilled him
through with jealousy to whomsoever addressed,
because it revealed to him that she had never felt
for him that which prompted its soft and trusting
sweetness—the smile which had fired all the evil
passions in his exceptionally evil nature — had
shown Gilbert a far more terrible truth: she had

never given him such a smile. *Soit.* He had had
such as he had cared for, and he was tired of them,
and done with them, and as bright and beautiful
were to be had for love or money, particularly for
money. Thus he might have thought, half in consoling earnest, half in mortification, and acted on
the reassuring argument. But the smile, the unknown smile, which had not lighted her face upon
their bridal day, which had never adorned the
happiest hour—and they had had some happy
hours—of their marriage, had beamed upon the
man whom of all men living Gilbert Lloyd hated
most bitterly—and that man was his brother. His
brother, Miles Challoner, their dead father's
darling son—(and when Lloyd thought of his
father his face was horrible to see, and his heart
was foul with curses and unnatural hate, for he
hated his dead father more than his living brother),—the heir who had been his rival always,
his master in their nursery, the object of his bit-
terest envy and enmity when he was so young
that it was a mystery of the devil how such
passions could have a place in his childish heart.

In the name of the devil, — in whom Gilbert
Lloyd was almost tempted to believe as he watched
that smile, and felt the tempest rise in his heart,
like the waves under the moonbeams,—how had
this complication come about! This he could
readily ascertain, but what would it avail him
to know it? If she loved this hated brother of
his, what could he do? Enjoy the hideous revenge of keeping quiet, and letting their mutual
love grow into the blessing and hope of their existence perhaps, and then come forward and expose
all the truth, and crush the two at once? And
then? His own share in this, what would it be?
Utter ruin; and for his brother the sympathy of
the world! To be sure it would be deep disgrace
for the woman who, secretly a wife, encouraged a
man to love, and to hope to win her; but she
could deny her love and the encouragement, and
nobody could prove either, and she was entirely
ignorant of the relation subsisting between Miles
Challoner and him. Of this Gilbert Lloyd did
not feel a moment's doubt. Miles would not di-
vulge a fact in which a terrible family secret was

involved, to anyone; he had taken his line towards
Gilbert on their first accidental meeting far too
decidedly for the existence of any doubt on that
point. If, on the other hand, Gilbert Lloyd were
to yield to the promptings of passion and revenge,
and betray the relationship, ruin of a double kind
would inevitably overtake him; vague indeed as
to its source or manner, but not admitting of any
doubt. He knew that such would be the case,
thus : One communication only had been addressed
to the man who is here called Gilbert Lloyd, by
his father, after his sudden departure from Rowley
Court. It was brief, and contained in the following words :   .

*" I have placed in the hands of a friend in whom
I have entire confidence the narrative of the events
which have ended with your banishment from my
house, and your erasure from our family annals for
ever. This friend is not acquainted with your personal appearance, and cannot therefore recognise you,
should your future conduct enable you to present
yourself in any place where he may be found; but he
will be in close and constant intercourse with my son;*

and should you venture, either directly or remotely, to injure my son, in person, reputation, estate, or by any means whatever, this friend, being warned by me to investigate any such injury done to my son, on the presumption that it comes from you, will be enabled to identify you; and is, in such case, bound to me by a solemn promise to expose the whole of the facts, and the proofs in his possession, in such manner as he may judge best for bringing you most certainly and expeditiously to that punishment which human weakness has prevented my being the means of inflicting upon you. I give you this information and warning, in the interest of my son, and also because I desire to turn you, by the only motive available for my purpose, from the commission of a crime whose penalty no one's weakness will enable you to evade."

Gilbert Lloyd had never been able during all the vicissitudes of his career—in all its levities, its successes, its failures, its schemes—to forget the warning, or even the phrasing, of this terrible letter. He had burned it in a fury which would have hardly been assuaged by the blood of the writer, and had tried to persuade himself after-

wards that he scoffed at the suspicions and the
threat and the precaution alike. But the effort
failed: he did not scoff—he believed and feared,
and remembered; and in this strange and ominous
complication, which had brought his brother across
his path under circumstances which any man
might have feared, he felt the futility of his pretended indifference to an extent which resembled
terror.

He wondered at himself now, when he remembered that whenever he had thought about
his wife at all in the early days after their separation, in the few and scattered speculations which
had arisen in his mind about her, the idea of her
ever loving another man had found no place. So
intense was his egotism, that, though he did not
indulge in the mere vanity of believing that she
still loved *him*, and would repent the step she had
taken, he did not in the least realise her matter-of-
fact emancipation from the ties which they loosed
by mutual consent. He had sometimes wondered
whether she got on well with her liberty and her
hundred pounds; whether she had gone back to

the drudgery of school-life, in the intensified form that drudgery assumes to a teacher; whether she had any friends, and how she accounted to them for her isolation; with other vague and placid vaticinations. But that this young and handsome woman, who had found out the unworthiness of her first love, had been rudely awakened from her woman's dream of happiness, and had exchanged all the sentiment with which she had regarded him for horror and contempt, and a steadily maintained purpose of utter separation — that she should have a second love, should dream again, never occurred to him. As little had he thought about the probability of his meeting her in the widely divergent course which his own life had taken from any within the previous experience of either. But he had met her; and one of the unexpected results of that undesirable event was to awaken him, with a shock, to the strongest suspicion that she did love and dream again, and that the object of the love and the dream was the man he most hated—was his brother. How Gilbert Lloyd would have regarded this circumstance, had he carried out his acceptation of the situation with such good faith and such complete indifference as Gertrude evinced, had he been able to see her again perfectly unmoved and without the slightest wish to alter anything in their position, he did not stop seriously to consider. This might have been; and for a minute or two his mind glanced at certain cynical possibilities in such a case, which might have enabled him to gratify his spite towards both his wife and his brother, in comparative security. But it was not; and that which was, absorbed him wholly.

Alternately raging against the feelings which possessed him, and arranging the facts of the case in order, and forcing himself to ponder them with his accustomed coolness, Gilbert Lloyd walked on for many miles without taking note of distance. When at length he bethought him of the time, and consulted his watch, he found he must hasten back to town, to be ready to dine with the "rich brute," who was to entertain a party of choice spirits devoted to the turf that day. The occasion was an important, and Gilbert Lloyd intended

that it should be a profitable, one. In the midst
of the anger and perturbation of his spirit, he was
quite capable of attending to his own and his
patron's interests—when they were identical; and
there was no mental process, involving no matter
what amount of passion or scheming or danger,
which Gilbert Lloyd could not lay aside—ranged
in its due place in his memory—to await its fitting
time; a valuable faculty, and not a little dangerous
in the possession of a man at war, more or less
openly, with society.

The next day, as Gilbert Lloyd, as usual admirably mounted, turned into the Park, and made
for the then almost deserted Lady's Mile, a carriage swept rapidly by. Two ladies occupied the
back-seat, and on the front Lloyd beheld the unusual apparition of Lord Sandilands. The ladies
were the Marchioness of Carabas and Miss Lambert. They saw him; and Lady Carabas gave
him a bow at once graciously graceful and deli-
ciously familiar; but Miss Lambert looked straight
before her with such exquisitely perfect unconsci-
ousness, that it never occurred to either of her

companions that she had recognised Gilbert Lloyd.

Then savage anger took possession of him once more, and scattered all the process of thought he had been going through to the winds, and he swore that, come what might, he would meet her where it would be impossible for her to avoid him.

CHAPTER VI.

GERTRUDE SPEAKS.

LORD TICEHURST'S attachment to the turf was by no means of a lukewarm or of a perfunctory character. He was not one of the young men of the present day, who keep a racing-stud as they keep anything else, merely for their amusement; who exult indecently when they are successful, who are even more indecently depressed when they are unfortunate. Having such a man as Gilbert Lloyd for his "confederate," manager, and agent, the young nobleman did not require to look into the details of his stud and his stable as he otherwise would have done; but nothing was ever done without his knowledge and approval, and his heart was as much bound up in turf-matters as it had been when, under the initiation of Plater Dobbs, he first made his

entrance into the Ring. Perhaps if this attachment to racing-matters and racing-men had been
less strong, Lord Ticehurst would have noticed
a certain change in Lloyd's manner towards him
which would have displeased him much. For,
notwithstanding that he struggled hard against
the display of any such feeling, there arose in
Gilbert's breast a sullen animosity, a dogged dislike to his friend and patron, which very often
would not be kept down, but came surging up
into his face, and showed itself in knit brows and
tightened lips, and hard cold insolence of bearing.
This was very different from the deep and bitter
hatred with which Gilbert Lloyd regarded Miles
Challoner, though it sprung from the same cause,
the admiration which each of them felt for Gertrude. In the present state of his feelings for
her, it enraged Gilbert to think that anyone
should dare to pay attention to one who had
been, who by the law still was, his property :
but the depth and measure of his hatred was
very much acted upon by the knowledge that
Lord Ticehurst was merely regarded by Gertrude

as one of a hundred hangers-on, while Miles Challoner stood in a very different position. But though this angry feeling from time to time got the better of Gilbert Lloyd's usually placid and equable temperament, and led to exhibitions of temper which he was afterwards frightened at and ashamed of, they were never noticed by the kindly-hearted, thick-headed young man whom he had in training, or, if they were, were ascribed to some of those "tighteners" and "botherations" which were supposed to fall naturally to "old Gilbert's" lot in transacting his business of the turf. "There's bad news up from the Pastures, I suppose," Lord Ticehurst would say to some of his friends, after the occurrence of some little episode of the kind; "old Gil's uncommon cranky this mornin', and no two ways about it. It's always best to leave him to come round by himself when he is in this way, so lets you and me go down to Rummer's and get some luncheon." But throughout all his annoyances, and the renovated passion for his wife,—passion of the strongest, wildest, most enslaving kind, was

now always present in his heart,—Gilbert Lloyd
held carefully to his business career, losing no
opportunity of showing himself of service to his
pupil, and taking every care that his pupil was
made aware of the fact.

"I say, Etchingham," said Gilbert one morning, glancing up from his accounts at his lordship,
who was moodily looking out of window, smoking,
and wondering whether he should propose to Miss
Lambert before the season finally broke up, or
leave it until next spring,—"I say, Etchingham
I'm pretty near sick of town."

"Same here!" replied his lordship; "fusty
and beastly, ain't it? Well, we're close upon
cutting it; it's Goodwood the week after next, and
then there's Brighton—"

"O, curse Brighton!" broke in Lloyd.

"All right," said Lord Ticehurst, lazily dropping into a chair. "Curse Brighton by all means.
But what a rum fellow you are! You wouldn't
go to the Brighton Meeting last year; and I
recollect that there was a talk about it at Rummer's; and Jack Manby—the Bustard, you know

—said you'd never go there again, since in Gaslight's year, I think he said, the sea-air spoiled your complexion."

"Manby's a chattering idiot," said Lloyd savagely; "and next time you hear men talking of why I don't go to the Brighton Meeting, you may say I don't go because it isn't a meeting at all, a third-rate concern with a pack of platers to run, and a crowd of cockneys to look at them. You may say that."

"Much obliged," said Lord Ticehurst; "you may say it yourself, if you want to. I don't hold with mixin' myself up in other fellows' shines;" and he sucked solemnly at his cigar, and did his best to look dignified.

"My dear old Etchingham, don't be angry. I was vexed at hearing you repeat the gabble of those infernal fellows at that filthy tavern—it isn't anything better—because it's not only about me they talk. However, that's neither here nor there. I suppose you'll have the wind-up dinner at Richmond as usual."

"All right, Gil, my boy!" said his good-

tempered lordship; "there's no bones broke, and
it's all squared. Of course we'll have the dinner.
Let's see," looking at his memorandum-book;
"Friday-week, how will that suit? Mrs. Stapleton Burge's party. O, ah, that's nothing!" he
added quickly, growing very red.

"Very well," said Gilbert quietly. "Friday-
week, since you've only got Mrs. Stapleton Burge's
party; and that's nothing, you say. Friday-week
will do. I'm to ask the usual lot, I suppose?"

"Yes, usual lot, and one or two more, don't
you think? It was deuced slow last time, I
remember. Only old Toshington to talk, and
everybody's tired of his old gab. Ask someone
to froth it up a bit, one of those writing-fellows
one sees at some houses, or an actor who can
mimic fellows, and that kind of thing, don't you
know?"

"I know," said Gilbert, by no means jumping
at the suggestion; "but I generally find that
your clever fellows who write are miserable unless
they have all the talk to themselves; and the
actors are insulted if you ask them to do any of

their hanky-panky, as though, by Jove, they'd be invited for anything else. However, I'll look up some of them, and do my best. Anybody else?"

"No, I think not. Unless, by the way, you were to ask that man that my aunt's taken up lately—Challoner."

The name brought the blood into Gilbert's face, and he paused a moment before he said: "I don't think I'd have that fellow, Etchingham, if I were you."

"What's the matter with him? Ain't he on the square? Bad egg, and that kind of thing?"

"I know very little about him," said Gilbert, fixing his eyes on Lord Ticehurst's face; "nothing, indeed, for the matter of that; and he's never crossed me, and never will have the opportunity. I said, 'if I were you.'"

"Yes, well—I know. Drop the riddle business and speak out. What do you mean?"

"Plainly, then, I've noticed — and I can't imagine how it has failed to escape you—that this man Challoner is making strong running for a

lady for whom I have heard you profess the
greatest admiration—Miss Lambert."

"O, ah, yes—thanks; all right," said Lord
Ticehurst, looking more foolish than usual—in
itself a stupendous feat; "well, I ain't spooney
particularly on Challoner, so you needn't ask
him."

Peers of the realm, and persons known as
"public characters," command more civility and
attention in England than anyone else. With
tradesmen, hotel-waiters, and railway-porters this
feeling is so strongly developed that they will
leave any customer to serve a great lord or a
popular comedian. Lord Ticehurst's name stood
very high at the Crown and Sceptre at Richmond,
not merely because he was an earl—they see
plenty of them during the season at the Crown
and Sceptre—but because he was freespoken,
lavish with his money, and "had no cussed pride
about him." Consequently, whenever he dined
there the dinner was always good, which is by no
means always the case at the C. and S.; and the

present occasion was no exception. There were about twenty guests, all men, and nearly all men of one set, who, though they were mostly well-born and, in the main, tolerably educated, apparently never sought for and certainly never attained any other society. The outside world was familiar with their names, through seeing them printed in the newspapers as attending the various great race-meetings; and with their personal appearance, through seeing them at Tattersall's and in the Park, especially on Sundays in the season. Some had chambers in the Albany, some in smaller and cheaper sets; many of them lived humbly enough in one bedroom in the lodging-house-swarming streets round St. James's; all of them haunted Rummer's in Conduit-street; and most of them belonged to some semi-turf, semi-military, whole card-and-billiard-playing club. Some of them were believed to be married, but their wives were never seen with them by any chance; for they never went into society, to the opera or the theatres; and they were always put into the bachelor quarters at country-houses, and into the

topmost rooms at the hotels, where they treated
the female domestics in a pleasant and genial way,
a compound of the manners of the groom and the
commercial bagman.

They gathered in full force at the Crown and
Sceptre that lovely July afternoon; for they knew
that they would have a good dinner and wine
without stint. Captain Dafter was there—a little
wiry man with sandy scraps of whisker and a
mean little white face, but who was the best
amateur steeplechase rider in England, with limbs
of steel and dauntless pluck. Next to him sat
a fat, heavy-headed, large-jowled man, with a
face the shape and colour of an ill-baked quartern
loaf; a silent stupid-looking man, who ate and
drank enormously, and said, and apparently understood, nothing; but who was no less a personage
than the " Great Northern," as he was called,
from having been born at Carlisle; the enormous
bookmaker and King of the Ring, who began life
as a plumber with eighteenpence, and was then
worth hundreds of thousands. There, too, with
his neatly-rolled whiskers and his neatly-tied blue

bird's-eye scarf, with its plain solid gold horse-shoe pin, was Dolly Clarke, the turf-lawyer. Years ago Dolly would have thought himself lucky if he ever made six hundred a-year. Six thousand is now nearer Dolly's annual income, all brought about by his own talent, and "not standing on any repairs," as he put it, a quality which is to be found in the dictionary under the word " unscrupulousness ;" for when old Mr. Snoxell, inventor of the Pilgrim's-Progress Leather for tender feet, died, and left all his money to his son Sam, who had been bred to the law, Sam took Dolly Clarke into partnership, and by combining shrewdness with bill-discounting, and a military connection with a knowledge of turf-matters, they did a splendid business. You would almost mistake Dolly Clarke for a gentleman now, and Samuel Snoxell calls all the army by their Christian names. Next to Dolly Clarke was Mr. Bagwax, Q.C., always retained in cases connected with the turf, and rather preferring to be on the shaky and shady side, which affords opportunities for making great fun out of would-be-honest wit-

nesses, and making jokes which, of all the persons
in court, are not least understood by Mr. Justice
Martingale, who knows a horse from a wigblock,
and is understood to have at one time heard the
chimes at midnight. The redoubtable Jack Manby, called "the Bustard," because in his thickness
of utterance he was in the habit of declaring that
he "didn't care about bustard so long as he got
beef," was there; and old Sam Roller the trainer,
looking something like a bishop, and something
more like Mr. Soapey Sponge's friend, Jack
Spraggon; and a tall thin gentlemanly man, who
looked like a barrister, and who was " Haruspex,"
the sporting prophet of the *Statesman*. Nor had
Gilbert Lloyd forgotten his patron's hint about
the enlivening of the company by the representa-
tives of literature and the drama. Mr. Wisbottle,
the graphic writer, the charming essayist, the
sparkling dramatist; Wisbottle, who was always
turning up in print when you least expected him;
Wisbottle, of whom his brilliant friend and toady
M'Boswell had remarked that he had never teti-
gited anything which he hadn't ornavited;—Wis-

bottle represented literature, and represented it in a very thirsty and talkative, not to say flippant, manner. As the drama's representative, behold Mr. Maurice Mendip, a charming young fellow of fifty-five, who, in the old days of patent theatres and great tragedians, would have alternated Marcellus with Bernardo, playing Horatio for his benefit, when his landlady, friends, and family from Bermondsey came in with tickets sold for his particular behoof, but who, in virtue of loud lungs and some faint reminiscence of what he had seen done by his betters, played all the "leading business" in London when he could get the chance, and was the idolised hero of Californian gold-diggers and Australian aborigines. He was, perhaps, a little out of place at such a party, being heavy, grave, and taciturn; but most people knew his name, and when told who he was, said, "O, indeed!" and looked at him with that mixture of curiosity and impertinence with which "public characters" are generally regarded. The other guests were men more or less intimately connected with the turf, who talked to each other in a low grumbling monotone, and whose whole desire was to get the better of each other in every possible way.

The dinner, which had called forth loud encomiums, was over; the cigars were lighted, and the conversation had been proceeding briskly, when in a momentary lull Dolly Clarke, who had the reputation for being not quite too fond of Gilbert Lloyd, said in a loud voice: "Well, my lord, and after Goodwood comes Brighton, and of course you hope to be as lucky there."

"We've got nothing at Brighton," replied Lord Ticehurst, looking uneasily towards where Gilbert was occupying the vice-chair.

"Nothing at Brighton!" echoed Dolly Clarke, very loud indeed; "why, how's that?"

"Because we don't choose, Mr. Clarke," said Gilbert, from the other end of the table—he had been drinking more than his wont, and there was a strained, flushed look round his eyes quite unusual to him—"because we don't choose; I suppose that's reason enough."

"O, quite," said Dolly Clarke, with a short

laugh. "I spoke to Lord Ticehurst, by the way; but in your case I suppose it's not an 'untradesmanlike falsehood' if you represent yourself as 'the same concern.' However, you used to go to Brighton, Lloyd."

"Yes," replied Gilbert quickly, "and so used you, when you were Wiggins and Proctor's outdoor clerk at eighteen shillings a-week—by the excursion-train! Times have changed with both of us."

"Lloyd had him there, Jack," whispered Bagwax, Q.C., to his neighbour the Bustard. "Impudent customer, Master Clarke! I recollect well when he used to carry a bag and serve writs, and all that; and now—"

"Hold on a binnit," said the Bustard; "he's an awkward customer is Clarke, and he'll show Gilbert no bercy." And, indeed, there was a look in Mr. Dolly Clarke's ordinarily smiling, self-satisfied face, and a decision in the manner in which his hand had, apparently involuntarily, closed upon the neck of the claret-jug standing in front of him, that augured ill for the peace of the party in

general, or the personal comfort of Gilbert Lloyd
in particular. But old Sam Roller's great spec-
tacles had happened to be turned towards the turf-
lawyer at the moment; and the old fellow, seeing
how matters stood, had telegraphed to Lord Ticehurst, while Mr. Wisbottle touched Clarke's knee
with one hand under the table, and removed the
claret-jug from his grasp with the other, whispering, "Drop it, dear old boy! What's the good?
You kill him, and have to keep out of the way,
and lose all the business in Davies-street. He
kills you, and what becomes of the policies for the
little woman at Roehampton? Listen to the
words of Wisbottle the preacher, my chick, and
drop it." And it having by this time dawned
upon Lord Ticehurst that there was something
wrong, that young nobleman cut into the conversation in a very energetic and happy manner,
principally dilating upon the necessity of his guests
drinking as much and as fast as they possibly
could. The first part of the proposition seemed
highly popular, but certain of the company objected to being hurried with their liquor, and de-

manded to know the reason of their being thus pressed. Then Lord Ticehurst explained that he was under the necessity of putting in an appearance that night at the house of a very particular friend, where an evening party was being held; that it was an engagement of long-standing, and one which it was impossible for him to get off. This, he added, need be no reason for breaking up their meeting; he should only be too delighted if they would stop as long as they pleased; and he was quite sure that his worthy vice would come up to that end of the table, and fill his place much more worthily than it had hitherto been filled.

But to this proposition there was a great deal of demur. Several of the guests, keen men of business, with the remembrance of the morrow's engagements and work before them, and having had quite sufficient wine, were eager to be off. Others, who would have remained drinking so long as any drink was brought, scarcely relished their cups under the presidency of Gilbert Lloyd, who was regarded by them as anything but a convivialist; while others, again, had engagements in

town which they were anxious to fulfil. Moreover, the plan proposed by his patron was anything but acceptable to Gilbert Lloyd himself.
Ordinarily almost abstemious, he had on this occasion taken a great deal of wine, and, though he
was by no means intoxicated, his pulses throbbed
and his blood was heated in a manner very unusual with him. From the first moment of Ticehurst's mentioning that he was going on this
evening to a party at Mrs. Stapleton Burge's
house, Gilbert felt convinced, by his friend's manner, that he must have some special attraction
there, and that that attraction must be the presence of Gertrude. This thought — the feeling
that she would be there, surrounded by courtiers
and flatterers — worried and irritated him, and
every glass of wine which he swallowed increased
his desire to see her that night. What matter if
he had been rebuffed! That was simply because
he had not had the chance of speaking to her.
Give him that opportunity, and she would tell a
very different tale. He should have that opportunity if he met her face to face in society; it

would be impossible for her, without committing a
palpable rudeness—and Gilbert Lloyd knew well
that she would never do that—to avoid speaking
to him. *Château qui parle est pret de se rendre.*
A true proverb that; and he made up his mind to
tell Lord Ticehurst to take him to Mrs. Stapleton
Burge's gathering, and to run his chance with
Gertrude.

So that when he heard his patron propound
that he should remain behind, to fan into a flame
the expiring embers of an orgie which, even at its
brightest, had afforded him no amusement, his
disgust was extreme, and uncomplimentary as
they were to himself, he fostered and repeated the
excuses which he heard on all sides. Nor did he
content himself with passive resistance, but went
straight to Lord Ticehurst, and taking him aside,
told him that this was, after all, only a " duty
dinner;" that all that was necessary had been
done, and it was better they should break up then
and there. "Moreover," said he, "I've a fancy
to go with you to-night. You're always telling
me I don't mix enough in what you call society;

and as this is the end of the season, and we're not likely to be—well, I was going to say bothered with women's parties for a long time, I don't mind going with you; in fact, I should rather like it. These fellows have done very well, and we can now leave them to shift for themselves." Lord Ticehurst's astonishment at this suggestion from his Mentor was extreme. "What a queer chap you are, Gil!" he said; "when I've asked you to go to all sorts of houses, first-class, where everything is done in great form and quite correct, you've stood out and fought shy, and all that kind of thing. And now you want to go to old Mother Burge's,—old cat who stuffs her rooms with a lot of people raked up from here and there! 'Pon my soul there's no knowing where to have you, and that's about the size of it!" But in this matter, as in almost every other, the young man gave way to his friend, and the party broke up at once; and Lord Ticehurst and Gilbert Lloyd drove home to Hill-street, dressed themselves, and proceeded to Mrs. Stapleton Burge's reception.

Mrs. Stapleton Burge lived in a very big house in Great Swaffham-street, close out of Park-lane, and though a very little black-faced woman herself, did everything on a very large scale. Her footmen were enormous creatures, prize-fed, big-whiskered, ambrosial; her chariot was like a family ark; the old English characters in which her name and address were inscribed surged all over her big cards. She had a big husband, a fat fair man with a protuberant chest, and receding forehead, and little eyes, who was a major in some Essex yeomanry, and who was generally mistaken by his guests for the butler. Everybody went to Mrs. Stapleton Burge's; and she, sometimes accompanied by the major, but more frequently without him, went everywhere. Nobody could give a reason for either proceeding. When the Stapleton Burges went out of town at the end of the season, nobody knew where they went to. Some people said to the family place in Essex, but Tommy Toshington said that was all humbug; he'd looked up the county history, and there wasn't any such place as Fenners; and he, Tommy,

thought they either retired to the back of the
house in Great Swaffham-street, or took lodgings
at Ramsgate. But the next season they appeared
again, as blooming and as big as ever. Lord
Ticehurst, in his description of Mrs. Burge's
parties, scarcely did that worthy woman justice.
People said, and truly, that those gatherings were
"a little mixed;" but Lady Tintagel took care
that some of the very best people in London were
seen at them. If Mrs. Burge would have her
own friends, that, Lady Tintagel said, was no
affair of hers. Mrs. Burge swore by Lady Tintagel, and the major swore at her. "If it wasn't
for that confounded woman," he used to say, "we
shouldn't be going through all this tomfoolery,
but should be living quietly at—" He was never
known to complete the sentence. Lady Tintagel
was Mrs. Burge's sponsor in the world of fashion,
and the major lent money to Lord Tintagel, who
was an impecunious and elderly nobleman. When
Lady Tintagel presided over a stall at an aristo-
cratic fancy-fair for the benefit of a charity, Mrs.
Burge furnished the said stall, and took Lady

Tintagel's place thereat during the dull portion of the day. Lady Tintagel's celebrated *tableaux vivants* were held in Mrs. Burge's big rooms in Great Swaffham-street, the Tintagel establishment being carried on in a two-roomed house in Mayfair. Mrs. Burge "takes" Lady Tintagel to various places of an evening, when the Tintagel jobbed horses are knocked up, and never has "her ladyship" out of her mouth.

When Lord Ticehurst and Gilbert Lloyd arrived at the hospitable mansion, they found the rooms crowded. It was a great but trying occasion for Mrs. Burge — trying, because it was plainly the farewell *fête* of the season; and all the guests were talking to one another of where they were going to, while she, poor woman, had a dreary waste of seven months before her, to be passed away from the delights of fashionable life. To how many people did she promise a speedy meeting at Spa, at Baden, in the Highlands, in Midland country-houses? and all her interlocutors placed their tongues in their cheeks, and knew that until the next summons of Parliament

drew the town together, and simultaneously produced a card of invitation from Mrs. Burge, they
should not meet their hostess of the night. Meantime, the success of the present gathering was
unimpeachable. Everybody who was left in London had rallied round Great Swaffham-street;
and there was no doubt but that the *Morning Post*
of the coming day would convey to the ends of
the civilised world a list of fashionables which
would redound in the most complete manner to
the *éclat* of Mrs. Stapleton Burge.

The necessary form of introduction had been
gone through—scarcely necessary, by the way, in
Great Swaffham-street; for the men always
averred that Mrs. Burge never knew half the
people at her own parties—and Lord Ticehurst,
having done his duty in landing Gilbert, had
strolled away among the other *convives*, with what
object Gilbert well enough knew. He, Gilbert
Lloyd, had rather a habit of trusting to chance in
matters of this kind; and, on the present occasion,
he found that chance befriended him. For while
his patron, eager and anxious-eyed, went roaming

round the room in hot search for the object of his
thoughts, Gilbert, no less anxious, no less determined, remained quietly near the entrance-door,
and narrowly watched each passing face. He
knew most of them. A London man of half-
a-dozen seasons can scarcely find a fresh face in
any evening party on which he may chance to
stumble. We go on in our different sets,
speaking to every other person we meet, and familiar with the appearance of all the rest—what
freshness and variety! Some of the passers-
by raised their eyebrows in surprise at seeing
Lloyd in such a place; others nodded and smiled,
and would have stopped to speak but for the plain
noli-me-tangere expression which he wore. He
returned the nods and grins in a half-preoccupied,
half-sullen manner, and it was not until he heard
Miles Challoner's voice close by him that he
seemed thoroughly roused. Then he drew back
from the door-post, against which he had been
leaning, and ensconcing himself behind the broad
back of a stout old gentleman, his neighbour, saw
Gertrude enter the room, on Miles Challoner's

arm. They had been dancing; she was flushed and animated, and looked splendidly handsome, as evidently thought her companion. Her face was upturned to his, and in her eyes was a frank, honest look of love and trust, such a look as Gilbert Lloyd recollected to have seen there when he first knew her years ago, but which had soon died out, and had never reappeared until that moment. And it was for Miles Challoner that her spirits had returned, her love and beauty had been renewed; for Miles Challoner, whom he hated with a deadly hate, who had been his rock ahead throughout his life, and who was now robbing him of what indeed he had once thrown aside as valueless, but what he would now give worlds to repossess. Gilbert Lloyd's face, all the features of which were so well trained and kept in such constant subjection, for once betrayed him, and the evil passion gnawing at his heart showed itself in his fiery eyes, surrounded by a strained hot flush, and in his rigidly set mouth. Tommy Toshington, tacking about the room to avoid the pressure of the crowd, and coming suddenly round

Lloyd's stout neighbour, was horrified by the expression in Gilbert's face.

"Why, what's the matter, Lloyd, my boy?" asked the old gentleman; "you look quite ghastly, by Jove! Ellis's claret not disagreed with you, has it?"

"Not a bit of it, Tommy; I'm all right," said Gilbert with an effort; "room's a little hot— perhaps that's made me look a little white."

"Look a little white! Dammy, you looked a little black when I first caught sight of you. You were scowling away at somebody; I couldn't make out who."

"Not I," said Gilbert, with an attempt at a laugh; "I was only thinking of something."

"O, shouldn't do that," said Mr. Toshington; "devilish stupid thing thinking; never comes to any good, and makes a fellow look deuced old. Lots of people here to-night;" then looking round and sinking his voice, "and rather a mixture, eh? I can't think where some of the people come from; one never sees them anywhere else." And the old gentleman, whose father had been a dissenting hatter at Islington, propped his double gold-eyeglass on his nose, and surveyed the company with a look of excessive *hauteur*.

"See!" he said presently, nudging Gilbert with his elbow; "you reck'lect what I told you, down at the Crystal Palace that day, about Etchingham and Miss What-do-you-call-'em, the singer?—that it wasn't any go for my lord, because there was another fellow cutting in in that quarter—you reck'lect? Well, look here, here they are,—What's-his-name, Chaldecott or something, and the girl."

"I see them," said Lloyd, drawing back.

"All right," said Toshington; "you needn't hide yourself; don't you be afraid, they're much too much taken up with each other to be looking at us. Gad, she's a devilish pretty girl, that, ain't she, Lloyd? There's a sort of a something about her which—such a deuced good style too, and way of carryin' herself! Gad, as to most of the women now—set of dumpy little brutes!—might be kitchen-maids, begad!"

"Just look, Toshington, will you? I can't

see, for this old fool's shoulder's in the way. Has Challoner left Miss Lambert?"

"Yes, he's stepped aside to speak to Lady Carabas; Miss Lambert is standing by the mantelpiece, and—"

"All right, back in half-a-second!" and made straight for the place where Gertrude was standing.

"Now, that's a funny thing!" said old Toshington to himself, as he looked after him. "What does that mean? Is Lloyd making the running for his master, or is that a little commission on his own account? No go either way, I should say; the man in the beard means winning there, and no one else has a chance."

As Gilbert Lloyd crossed the room, Gertrude looked up, and their eyes met. The next instant she looked round for Miles Challoner, but he was still busily engaged in talking to Lady Carabas. Then she saw some other ladies of her acquaintance, seated within a little distance, and she determined on crossing the room to them. But she had scarcely moved a few steps when Gilbert

Lloyd was by her side. Gertrude's heart beat rapidly; she scarcely heard the first words of salutation which Gilbert uttered; she looked quickly round and saw that, though Miles was still standing by Lady Carabas's chair, his eyes were fixed on her and Lloyd. What could she do? What is that her husband says?

"Too much of this fooling! You *must* hear me now!"

With an attempt at a smile, Gertrude turned to her persecutor and said, "Once for all, leave me!"

"I will not," said he, in a low voice, but also with a smile on his face. "You cannot get away from me without exciting the suspicion, or the wonder at least, of the room. How long do you imagine I am going to let this pretty little play proceed? How long am I to look on and see the puppets dallying?"

Gertrude flushed scarlet as he said these words, but she did not speak.

"You're carrying this business with too high a hand," said he, emboldened by her silence. "You seem to forget that I have a word or two to say in the matter."

"See, Gilbert Lloyd," said Gertrude, still smiling and playing with her fan, "you sought me; not I you. Go now, and—"

"Go!" said Gilbert, who saw Miles Challoner looking hard at them,—"go, that he may come! Go! You give your orders freely! What hold have you on me that I am to obey them?"

"Would you wish me to tell you?"

"Tell away!" said Lloyd defiantly. "I don't mind."

"Here, then," said Gertrude, beckoning him a little closer with her fan, then whispering behind it. But one short sentence, a very few words, but, hearing them, Gilbert Lloyd turned death-white, and felt the room reel round before him. In an instant he recovered sufficiently to make a bow, and to leave the room and the house. When he got out into the street, the fresh air revived him; he leaned for a moment against some railings to collect his thoughts; and as he moved off, he said aloud, "He *did* suspect it, then; and he told her!"

CHAPTER VII.

HALF-REVEALED.

OF all the places on which the autumnal moon, approaching her full like a comely matron, looks down, there are many far less picturesque and less enjoyable than that bit of Robertson-terrace, St. Leonards, which adjoins the narrow strip of beach communicating with the old town of Hastings proper.   On this beach the moonbeams play

> "Among the waste and lumber of the shore,
>   Hard coils of cordage, swarthy fishing-nets,
>   Anchors of rusty fluke, and boats updrawn,"

casting grim and fantastic shadows, and bringing oddest objects into unwonted and undue prominence.   Robertson-terrace—as hideous, architecturally considered, as are the majority of such marine asylums for the temporary reception of Londoners —stands back from the road, and has its stuccoed proportions somewhat softened by the trees and shrubs in the "Enclosure," as the denizens love to call it, a small oblong strip of something which ought to be green turf, but what, under the influence of promenading and croquet-playing, has become brown mud. In the moonlight on this lovely night in early autumn, some of the denizens yet linger in the Enclosure. Young people mostly, of both sexes, who walk in pairs, and speak in very low tones, and look at each other with very long immovable glances; young people who cannot imagine why people ever grow old, who cannot conceive that there can be any pleasure except in that one pastime in which they themselves are then employed—who cannot conceive, for instance, what enjoyment that old gentleman, who has been so long seated in the drawing-room balcony of No. 17, can find in life.

That old gentleman is Lord Sandilands, who, the London season over, has come down to St. Leonards for a little sea-air, and quiet and change. One reason for his selection of St. Leonards is that Miss Grace Lambert and Mrs. Bloxam are staying

within a few miles' distance, at Hardriggs, Sir
Giles Belwether's pretty place. Lord Sandilands
had been invited to Hardriggs, also, but he dis-
liked staying anywhere except with very intimate
friends; and, moreover, he had come to that time
of life when rest was absolutely essential to him,
and he knew that under Sir Giles Belwether's
ponderous hospitality he would simply be moving
the *venue* of his London life without altering any
of its details. Moreover, the old gentleman, by
coming to St. Leonards, was carrying out a kindly
scheme long since laid, of giving Miles Challoner
occasional opportunities of seeing Miss Lambert.
Miles was not invited to stay at Hardriggs; he did
not even know Sir Giles Belwether; but he became Lord Sandilands' guest in the lodgings in
Robertson-terrace, and, as such, he was taken over
by his friend to Hardriggs, introduced to the host,
and received with the greatest hospitality. Lord
Sandilands has this advantage over the youthful
promenaders in the "Enclosure," that while they
cannot imagine what he is thinking of, he perfectly
well divines the subject of their thoughts, and is

allowing his own ideas to run in another vein of that special subject. He has just made Miles confess his love for Grace Lambert, and all the drawbacks and disadvantages of the position are opening rapidly before him.

"I might have expected it," said the old gentleman half-aloud; "I knew it was coming. I saw it growing day by day, and yet I never had the pluck to look the affair straight in the face—to make up my mind whether I'd tell him anything about Gertrude's parentage; and I don't know what to do now. Ah, here he is!—Well, Miles, had your smoke? Lovely night, eh?"

"A lovely night, indeed! No end of people out by the sea."

"You wouldn't mind a turn in that lime-walk at Hardriggs just now, Miles, eh? with—Kate Belwether, or someone else?"

"Rather the someone else, dear old friend. And so you weren't a bit astonished at what I told you to-day?"

"Astonished, my boy! I astonished? Why, where do you think my eyes have been? I de-

clare you young fellows think that to you alone
has been confided the appreciation of beauty and
the art of love!"

"Anyone who imagines that must have ears,
and hear not, so far as your lordship is concerned,"
said Miles, laughing. "Now, of John Borlase,
commonly known as Baron Sandilands, the ladies
whom he courted and the conquests which he
made, are they not written in the *Chronique Scan-
daleuse* of the period?"

"Well, I don't know that. I'm of an old-
fashioned school, which holds that no gentleman
should so carry on his *amourettes* that the world
should talk about them. But the idea of your
thinking that I should be astonished when you
told me that you were head over ears in love
with—with Miss Lambert! *Nourri dans le sérail
j'en connais les détours,* Master Miles."

"And if not astonished, you were also not
annoyed?"

"Annoyed! Not the least bit in the world.
I don't mean to say that the matter looks to
me entirely one of plain-sailing, my dear boy;

there are certain difficulties which will naturally arise."

"Do you think that Grace's friends will make any obstacle? By the way, my dear lord, do you know anything of Miss Lambert's relations? I have never heard of or seen any connection but Mrs. Bloxam; but you who are so intimate with the young lady will probably know all about them."

A half-comic look of embarrassment over-shadowed Lord Sandilands' face as he heard this inquiry, and he waited for a moment before he replied, "Not I, indeed, my dear Miles; Miss Lambert has never spoken to me of her relations —indeed, I understood from her that she was an orphan, left to Mrs. Bloxam's charge. I shouldn't think you need look for any objection to your marriage being made by the lady's friends."

"That is one point happily settled; then the world?"

"The what?"

"The opinion of the world."

"Ah, that's a very different matter! You're

afraid of what people will say about your marrying a singer ?"

" To you, dear old friend, I will confess candidly that I am. Not that I have any position, God knows, on the strength of which to give myself airs."

" My dear boy, that's where you mistake. If you *had* a position, you might marry not merely a charming and amiable and lovely girl like this, against whom no word ought to be uttered, but even a person without the smallest rag of reputation ; and the world would say very little about it, and would speedily be silenced. Look at—no need, however, to quote examples. What I have said is the fact, and you know it."

" I am forced to acknowledge the truth of your remark, but while acknowledging it, I shall not permit the fact to turn me from my purpose. If Miss Lambert will accept me for a husband, I will gladly risk all the tattle of all the old cats in Belgravia."

" Your sentiments do you credit, my dear boy," said the old nobleman with a smile, " though the juxtaposition of 'tattle' and 'cats' is scarcely happy. I've noticed that when people are in love, the arrangement of their sentences is seldom harmonious. I suppose you feel tolerably certain of Miss Lambert's answer to your intended proposal. You are too much a man of the present day to anticipate any doubt in the matter."

" I should not be worth Miss Lambert's acceptance if I had any such vanity; and I know you're only joking in ascribing it to me."

" I was only joking; but now seriously, do you fear no rivals? You see how very much the young lady is sought after. Are you certain that her preference is given to you?"

" As certain as a man can be who has not 'put it to the touch to win or lose it all,' by ascertaining positively."

" And there is no one you are absolutely jealous of?"

" No one. Well,—no, not jealous of,—there is one man whom I regard with excessive distrust."

" You don't mean Lord Ticehurst?"

" O, no ! Lord Ticehurst's manners are rough and odd; but he is a gentleman, and, I'm sure, would 'behave as such,' in every possible way, to Miss Lambert. Indeed, no duchess of his acquaintance can be treated with greater respect than she is by him. I would not say as much of the other man."

"Who is he ?"

Miles hesitated a moment before he said, " Lord Ticehurst's great friend, Mr. Gilbert Lloyd."

"Mr. Gilbert Lloyd !" repeated Lord Sandilands, with a low whistle—"that's a very different matter. I don't mind telling you, my dear Miles, that I have had an uncomfortable impression about that young man ever since the first night we met him at Carabas House. It's singular too; for I know no real harm of the man. His tastes and pursuits are not such as interest or occupy me ; though, of course, that is the case with scores of persons with whom I am acquainted, and towards whom I feel no such dislike. Very odd, isn't it ?"

Miles looked hard at his friend to see whether there were any latent meaning in the question; but seeing that Lord Sandilands was apparently speaking without any strong motive, he said:

"It is odd. Perhaps," he added, "it is to be accounted for by the feeling that this—Mr. Gilbert Lloyd is not a gentleman?"

"N-no, not that. Though the man, amongst his own set, has an air of turfy, horsey life which is hideously repellent, yet with other people he shows that he knows at least the *convenances* of society, and is not without traces of breeding and education. I fancy that in this case I am suffering myself to be influenced by my belief in physiognomy. The man has a decidedly bad face; deceit, treachery, and cruelty are written in the shifty expression of his sunken eyes, in his thin tightened lips."

"And you really believe this?" said Miles earnestly.

"I do; most earnestly. Depend upon it, Nature never makes a mistake. We may fail to read her properly sometimes, but she never errs.

And in this case her handwriting is too plain to admit of any doubt."

Miles shuddered. The old gentleman noticed it, and laid his hand kindly on his friend's knee; then he said:

"But, after all, there's no reason for us to fear him. You say that he has been somewhat marked in his attention to Grace?"

"More than marked. Did you not notice the other night at the house of that odd woman, Mrs. Burge—O, no, I forgot, you were not there; but it was just before we left town, and Miss Lambert had been dancing with me, and I had only left her for a minute when Lloyd went up and spoke to her."

"Well?"

"Of course I don't know what he said, but they both seemed to speak very earnestly, and after a very few moments he left her abruptly and hurried away."

"Well, I don't think that proceeding ought to cause you much disquietude, Master Miles. In all probability, from what you say, Miss Lambert was giving Mr. Lloyd his *congé*, or, at all events, saying something not very pleasant to him. Have you ever spoken to her about Lloyd?"

"Once or twice only."

"And what has she said about him?"

"She seems to have taken your view of the question, my dear old friend, for she spoke of him with cold contempt and irrepressible dislike, and begged me never to mention his name to her again."

"Really, then it seems to me that you have nothing to fear in that quarter. That this Mr. Lloyd is a dangerous man I am convinced; that he would be desperate in any matter in which he was deeply interested, I don't doubt; but he may be as desperate as he pleases if Grace dislikes him, and loves you. By the way, as that question is still a moot point, Master Miles," added the old gentleman with a sly look, "the sooner you get it settled, the better. We shall be driving over to Hardriggs to-morrow, and I should think you *might* find an opportunity of speaking to the lady in private. I know I would at your time of life, and under the circumstances. And if you want an elderly gooseberry-picker, you may command me."

But seeing that Miles Challoner's face wore a stern and gloomy expression, Lord Sandilands dropped the tone of *badinage* in which he had been speaking, and said with great earnestness and softness :

" There is something strangely wrong with you to-night, Miles; something which keeps crossing your mind and influencing your thoughts; something which I am convinced is apart from, and yet somehow connected with, the subject we have been discussing. I have no wish to pry into your secrets, my dear boy; no right and no desire to ask for any confidence which you may not feel disposed to give. But as, since the death of my dear old friend, I have always regarded myself as your second father, and as I have loved you as I would have loved a son, I cannot bear to see you in obvious grief and trouble without longing to share it, and to advise and help you."

There was a pathos in the old man's tone, no

less than in his words, which touched Miles deeply. He took his friend's hand and pressed it, and his eyes were filled with tears, and his voice trembled as he said:

" God knows, my dearest friend, how willingly I acknowledge the truth of all that you have just said, and how recognisant I am of all your affection and kindness. I *am* troubled and disturbed, but there is nothing in my trouble that need be hid from you; nothing, indeed, which your sympathy and counsel will not lighten and tend to disperse."

" That's right," said the old nobleman, brightening up again. " Come, what is this trouble ? You're not worried for money, Miles ?"

" No. I had an odd letter from my lawyers yesterday about some mortgage that Sir Thomas Walbrook is interested in, but I haven't gone into the matter yet. No, not money,—I wish it were only that !"

" What then ? You've not gone and mixed yourself up with any—any connection—you know what I mean—that you feel it necessary to break off before you propose to Miss Lambert ?"

"Not I, dear old friend; nothing of the sort. Though my trouble is caused by what I think the necessity of giving a full explanation on a very difficult and delicate matter, before I ask Grace to become my wife."

"In the name of fortune, what is it, then?" asked Lord Sandilands.

"Simply this," said Miles, his face resuming its grave expression; "you know that my father's life was overshadowed and his whole mental peace destroyed, at a period when he might reasonably have looked forward to much future enjoyment, by the conduct of my younger brother, Geoffrey?"

"Ah! now I begin to comprehend—"

"Wait, and hear me out. That conduct, the nature of which I never could learn, and do not know at this moment, blighted my father's life, and changed him from an open-hearted, frank, genial man, into a silent and reserved valetudinarian. For years and years Geoffrey's name was never mentioned in our house. I was brought up under strict orders never to inquire about him, directly or indirectly; and those orders I obeyed to the letter. Only when my father was on his deathbed—you recollect my being telegraphed for from your house, where I was staying? I spoke of Geoffrey. I asked why he had been sent away, what he had done—"

"Your father did not tell you?" interrupted Lord Sandilands eagerly.

"He did not, he would not. It was just before he expired; his physical prostration was great; all he could say was that Geoffrey was, and for ever must be, dead to me. He implored me, he commanded me with his dying breath, if ever I met my brother to shun him, to fly from him, to let nothing earthly induce me to know him or acknowledge him."

"Your poor father was right," said Lord Sandilands; "he could have said nothing else."

"Do you justify my father's severity?" cried Miles in astonishment. "Do you hold that he was right in dying in anger with one of his own children, and in bequeathing his anger to me, the brother of the man whom in his wrath he thus harmed?"

"I do; I do indeed."

"Do you tell me that any crime not punishable by law could justify such a sentence?—a sentence of excommunication from his home, from family love, from—"

"Stay, stay, Miles. Tell me, how has this subject cropped up just now? What has brought it into your thoughts?"

"Because, as a man of honour, I feel that I ought to tell Miss Lambert something at least—as much as I know—of the story before I ask her to be my wife. Because I would fain have told her that my father was harsh and severe to a degree in his conduct to Geoffrey."

"That is impossible; that you can never say. Listen, Miles; I know more of this matter than you suspect. I know every detail of it. Your father made me his confidant, and I know the crime which your brother attempted."

"You do?—the crime!"

"The crime. The base, dastardly, hideous crime, which rendered it impossible for your father to do otherwise than renounce his son, and bid you renounce your brother for ever."

"Ah, my God!" groaned Miles, burying his head in his hands.

"There is no reason to be so excited, my poor boy," said Lord Sandilands, laying his hand gently on him. "You need tell Grace nothing of this; and be sure that this wretched Geoffrey will never trouble you again. He is most probably dead."

"Dead!" shrieked Miles, raising his livid face and staring wildly at his friend. "He lives— here amongst us! I have seen him constantly; he has recognised me, I know. This man of whom we were just speaking,—this man whom you call Gilbert Lloyd,—is my younger brother, Geoffrey Challoner!"

CHAPTER VIII.

L'HOMME PROPOSE.

WHEN a man of Lord Ticehurst's character and disposition makes up his mind to achieve a certain result—in the turf slang of the day, "goes in for a big thing"—he is not easily thwarted, or, at all events, he does not give up his idea without having tried to carry it through. The indiscreet, illiterate, but by no means bad-hearted, young nobleman aforenamed had given himself up, heart and soul, to a passion for the opera-singer known to him as Miss Grace Lambert, and had gone through a psychological examination of his feelings, so far as his brain-power permitted, with the view of seeing how the matter lay, and what would be his best means for securing his ends. The notion of succeeding dishonourably had never entered his head, or at least had not remained there for a moment. In that knowledge of the world which comes, no one knows how, to persons who are ignorant of everything else — that *savoir faire* which is learned unconsciously, and which can never be systematically acquired—Lord Ticehurst was a proficient. He was not, as times go, an immoral man, certainly not a wicked one; but he lived in a loose set, and it did not arise from conscientious scruples that he had not "tried it on" that Grace Lambert should become his mistress. Such a result would have given him considerable *éclat* amongst his friends, and his religious notions were not sufficiently developed to make him shrink from taking such a step. He did *not* take it because he knew it would be useless; because he knew that any such offer would be ignominiously rejected; that he would be spurned from the door, and never permitted again to be in the society of the girl whom he really loved. There was only one way out of it—to offer her marriage. And then the question came, Did he really love her sufficiently for that, and was he prepared to stand the consequences?

Did he really love her? He thought he could put in an answer to that, by Jove! Did he really love her? You should ask old Gil about that! Old Gil knew more of him than anyone else; and he could tell you—not that he knew what it was, what was the reason of it, don't you know?—that for the whole of last season he had been an altered man. He knew that himself—he confessed it; he felt that he had not taken any proper interest in the stable, and that kind of thing; indeed, if he had not had old Gil to look after it, the whole thing would have gone to the deuce. He knew that well enough, but he could not help it. He had been regular spoons on this girl, and he was, and he should be to the end of the chapter, amen. That was all he had got to say about it. His life had been quite a different thing since he had known her. He had left off swearing, and all that cussed low language that he used to delight in once upon a time; and he'd got up early, because he thought there was a chance of meeting her walking in the Park (he had met her once, and solemnly walked between her and Mrs. Blox-

am for an hour without saying a word); and he
had cut the *ballet* and its professors, with whom
formerly he had very liberal relations. The *cory-
phées* and the little *rats*, whom he had been in the
habit of calling by their Christian names, who
knew him by the endearing abbreviation of
"Ticey," and to whom formerly he was delighted
to stand and talk by the hour, received the coldest
of bows from their quondam friend, as he stood
amongst the wings of the opera-scenery on the
chance of a word of salutation from the *prima
donna* as she hurried from her dressing-room on
to the stage. But that word and the glance at
her were enough. "It's no good," he used to
say; "it won't do after that. If I go away to
supper at old Chalkstone's, and find Bella Mar-
shall and Kate Herbert and half-a-dozen of the
T. R. D. L. *ballet* there, 'pon my soul it don't
amuse me when they put the lobster-claws at
the end of their noses; and I think Bagwax and
Clownington and old Spiff—well, damme, they're
old enough to know better, and they might think
about—well, I don't want to preach about what

we're all coming to, and what must be precious near for them."

A man of this kind thus hit suffers very severely. The novelty of the passion adds considerably to his pangs. The fact that he cannot speak out his hopes and wishes irritates and worries him. To throw the handkerchief is easy enough at the first start—becomes easier through frequent practice; but to win the prize is a very different matter. With a lady of his own rank it would have been much easier wooing; but with Grace, Lord Ticehurst felt himself placed at a double disadvantage. He had to assuage the rage of his friends at the honour he was doing her, and he had to prove to her that he was doing her no honour at all. The former, though a difficult, was the easier task. Lord Ticehurst knew his aunt, Lady Carabas, quite well enough to be aware that, though she was the first *grande dame* who had introduced Miss Lambert into society, and that though up to that minute she had been the young lady's most steadfast friend, she would be the very first to rail against the *mésalliance*, and do all she could

to cry down that reputation which she had so
earnestly vaunted. Others would follow suit at
once, and he and his wife would have to run the
gauntlet. IIis wife! Ah, that was just the point;
he would not care a rap if she were his wife, if he
had her brains and her beauty to help in winning
the game for him. But Lord Ticehurst's knowledge of the world was too great to permit him to
flatter himself thus far; he knew that he had
never received any substantial acknowledgment
from Miss Lambert; and he recollected, with a
very unpleasant twinge, what Gilbert Lloyd had
said about Miles Challoner's attentions in that
quarter—attentions received almost as favourably
as they were earnestly proffered, as Lord Ticehurst had had an opportunity of witnessing at
Mrs. Stapleton Burge's reception.

Young noblemen of large fortunes are not in
the habit of fighting with their inclinations and
wishes. Lord Ticehurst felt that he must do his
best to make this girl marry him—whether she
would or not, he felt was doubtful, and acknowledged the feeling to himself with an honest frank-

ness which was one of his best characteristics. He
bore away with him his dull, wearying heartache,
his "restless, unsatisfied longing," to Goodwood,
where it cankered the ducal hospitality, and made
him think but little of the racing-prizes which he
carried off. He bore it away with him to the
hotel at Eastbourne, where, pending the Don-
caster week, he and his friends had set up their
Lares and Penates, and were doing their best to
gain health and strength from the sea-breezes and
quiet, and make up for the ravages of the London
season.

Except in the desultory manner already nar-
rated, Lord Ticehurst had not revealed to his confederate the state of his feelings towards Miss
Lambert. He had said nothing positive to him
regarding what was now his fixed intention, of
proposing for that young lady's hand, and it is
probable he would have been consistently reticent
had not chance brought the confession about in
this way.

It was a splendid August morning, and the
two gentlemen were seated in the largest sitting-

room of the pretty hotel, with its bay window
overlooking the pleasant promenading crowd of
sea-side loungers, bathable children, bathed young
ladies with their limp hair hanging down their
backs, old gentlemen walking up and down with
mouths and nostrils wide open to inhale as much
ozone as possible during their stay, and the other
usual common objects of the sea-shore. Breakfast
was just over, and cigars had already been lighted.
The blue vapour came curling round the sides of
the sporting-print in which Gilbert Lloyd's head
and shoulders were enveloped, and mixed with
another blue vapour which stole over the more
massive folds of the *Times*, with which Lord Ticehurst was engaged.

A shout of " Hallo !" betraying intense astonishment, roused Gilbert from his perusal
of the vaticinations of " Calchas." " What
makes you hallo out like that? What is it?"
he asked.

" What is it ! O, nothing particular," replied
Lord Ticehurst; adding immediately, " By Jove,
though !"

"No, but I say, Etchingham, something must have roused you to make you give tongue. What was it, old boy? No more scratchings for the Leger?"

"No, something quite different to that. Well, look here, if you must know;" and his lordship lazily handed the paper to his friend, and pointed to a particular paragraph.

"Advertisement!" said Lloyd as he took it. "Now what the deuce can you find to interest you among the advertisements?" But the expression of his face changed as he saw, in large letters, the name of Miss Grace Lambert; and on further perusal he found that Mr. Boulderson Munns, whose noble style he immediately recognised, informed the British public that he had made arrangements with this distinguished *prima donna* for a tour during the winter months, in the course of which she would visit the principal cities in England, Ireland, and Scotland, accompanied by a *troupe* of distinguished talent, superintended by Mr. Munns himself, who would lend all the resources of the justly-celebrated band and *répertoire* of the Grand Scandinavian Opera-house to the success of the design.

Gilbert Lloyd, who had felt his colour ebb when he first saw his wife's name, read through the advertisement carefully, but said nothing as he laid the paper down.

"Have you read it?" asked Lord Ticehurst.

"I have."

"And what do you think of it?"

"Think of it! What should I think of it, except that it will probably be a profitable speculation for—for Miss Lambert, and certainly a profitable one for Munns?"

"Well but, I say, look here! It mustn't come off."

"What mustn't?"

"Why, this what's-its-name—tour!"

"Then it will be a bad thing for Munns. But, seriously, Etchingham, what on earth do you mean? What are you talking about?"

"Well, I mean that—that young lady, Miss Lambert, mustn't go flitting about the country."

"Why not? What have you to do with it?"

"Why, haven't I told you—don't you recollect, before Ascot and all that?—only you're so deuced dull, and think of nothing but—well, never mind. Don't you recollect my saying I intended to ask Miss Lambert to be my wife?" And Lord Ticehurst, whom the avowal and the unusual flux of words rendered a bright peony colour, glared at his Mentor in nervous trepidation.

Gilbert looked at him very calmly. The corners of his mouth twitched for an instant as he began to speak, but he was otherwise perfectly composed as he said, "I had forgotten; you must forgive me; the stable takes up so much of my time that I have scarcely leisure to look after your other amusements. O, you intend to propose for this young lady! Do you think she will accept you?"

"That's a devilish nice question to ask a fellow, that is. 'Pon my soul, I don't think there's another fellow in the world that would have had the—well, the kindness—to ask that. I suppose it will be all right; if I didn't, I shouldn't—"

"Shouldn't ask, eh? Well, I suppose not, and it was indiscreet in me to suggest anything different. What do you propose to do now?"

"Well, what do you think? Perhaps I'd better go up to town—deuced odd town will look at this time of year, won't it?—and see Miss Lambert, and make it all straight with her; and then go off and see old Munns, and tell him he'll have to give up his notion of the what's-its-name—the tour. He'll want to be squared, of course, and we must do it for him; but I shall leave you to arrange that with him."

"Of course; that will not be a difficult matter." Gilbert Lloyd waited a minute before he added, "But there is no necessity for you to go to London on this portentous matter. Miss Lambert is much nearer to you than you imagine."

"Much nearer! What the deuce do you mean?" asked Lord Ticehurst, looking round as if he expected to see Gertrude entering the room.

"Exactly what I say. I had a letter this morning from Hanbury; he's staying at Hardriggs, old Sir Giles Belwether's place, not a dozen miles from here; and he mentioned that Miss Lambert was a guest there too. Wait a minute; I'll read you what he says. No, never mind, it's only some nonsense about Lady Belwether's insisting on old Bel having a Dean to stay in the house at the same time to counteract the effect of the stage, and—"

"D—d impertinence!" muttered Lord Ticehurst. "I always did hate that Hanbury—sneering beast! O, about twelve miles from here, eh? Might drive over to luncheon? What do you say, Gil? Do us good, eh?"

"Do *you* good, very likely, Etchingham! At all events, if you have made up your mind to this course, it's the best and the most honourable way to bring it to an issue at once. And I'm not sure that this is not an excellent opportunity. You will find the lady unfettered by business, free from the lot of fribbles who are always butterflying about her in town, and have only to make your running. I can't go; I've got letters to write, and things to do, and must stop here."

Within half an hour Lord Ticehurst's phaeton came spinning round to the door of the hotel, and Gilbert, stepping out on to the balcony, saw him—got up to the highest pitch of sporting *négligé*——drive off amid the unsuppressed admiration of the bystanders. Then Lloyd walked back into the room and flung himself on a sofa, and lit a fresh cigar, and as he puffed at it, soliloquised, "What was that I saw on a seal the other day? *Quo Fata ducunt.* What a wonderful thing that they should have led to this; that they should have led me to being the most intimate friend of a man who is now gone off to propose to my wife! My wife! I wonder when I shall make up my mind as to what my real feelings are towards her. After years of indifference, of absolute forgetfulness, I see her, and fall madly in love with her again—so madly that I pursue her, plainly seeing it is against her will, and, like an idiot, give her the chance of saying that to me which makes me hate her worse than ever—worse even than when we parted, and I *did* hate her then. But I've a feeling now which I had not during all that long interval of our separation. Then I did not care where she was, or what she did. Now, by the Lord, if I were to think that she cared for any man—or not that, I. know she does, curse him ! I know she does care for that man—I mean, if she were to give any man the position that was mine —that was ? that *is*, when I choose to claim it— he and I would have to settle accounts. That poor fool has no chance. Gertrude has no ambition—that's a fault I always found in her; if she had had, we might have risen together; but she was nothing when she was not sentimentally spoony; and she would throw over my lord, who really loves her in a way that I never thought him capable of, the title, money, and position, for the *beaux yeux* and the soft speeches of my sweet brother. What will be the end of that, I wonder ? By heavens, if I saw *that* culminating — if I thought that she was going to claim the freedom we agreed upon for the sake of bestowing herself on *him*, I'd stand the whole racket, run the whole risk, declare myself and my position openly, and let her do her worst !" He rose from the sofa and

walked to the window, where he stood looking out
for a few moments, then returned to his old position. "The worst, eh? How I hate that cursed
sea, and the glare of the sun on the cliffs! It
always reminds me of that infernal time. Do her
worst! She's the most determined woman I ever
saw. I shall never forget the look of her face that
night, nor the tone of her voice as she whispered
behind her fan. Well, sufficient for the day, &c.
That's to be met when it comes. It hasn't come
yet. I may be perfectly certain what reply will
be given to my dear young friend Etchingham,
who has just started on his precious fool's-errand;
and as for the other man—well, he's not staying
at Hardriggs, or Hanbury would have mentioned
him. There will be this country tour to fill up
the winter; and by the time next season arrives,
he may be off it, or she may be off it, or a
thousand things may have happened, which are
now not worth speculating about, but which will
serve my turn as they come." And Gilbert Lloyd
turned to his writing-desk, and plunged into calculations and accounts with perfectly clear brains,

in the working of which the thoughts of the previous half-hour had not the smallest share.

Meanwhile, Lord Ticehurst sat upright in his mail-phaeton, driving the pair of roans which were the cynosure of the Park during the season, and the envy of all horsey men always, through some of the loveliest scenery in Sussex. Not that scenery, except Grieve's or Beverley's, made much impression on his lordship. Constant variety of hill and dale merely brought out the special qualities and paces of the roans; wooded uplands suggested good cover-shooting; broad expanse of heath looked very like rabbits. To such a thorough sportsman thoughts like these occurred involuntarily; but he had plenty beside to fix what he called his mind. Though he had made as light as possible to his henchman of the expedition on which he was engaged, and given himself the airs of a conquering hero, he was by no means so well satisfied of his chances of success, or of his chances of happiness, were success finally achieved. His chances of success occupied him first. Well, he did not know—you could never tell about

women, at least he couldn't, whether they meant
it, or whether they didn't. He didn't know;
she was always very friendly, and that kind of
thing; but with women that went for nothing.
They'd draw you on, until you thought nothing
could be more straight; and then throw you over,
and leave you nowhere. N-no; he couldn't recollect anything particular that Miss Lambert had
ever said to induce him to hope: she'd admired
the roans as the groom moved them up and down
in front of her windows; and she'd said more than
once that she was glad some song of hers had
pleased him, and that was all. Not much indeed;
but then he was an earl; and the grand, undying
spirit of British flunkydom had led him to believe,
as indeed it leads every person of his degree to
believe, that "all thoughts, all passions, all delights, whatever stirs this mortal frame," are at
the command of anyone named in *Debrett*, or
eulogised by Sir Bernard Burke: "Ticehurst,
Earl of, Viscount Etchingham, b. 1831, succeeded
his father the 3d Earl in," &c. &c. What was
the use of that, if people were not to bow down in

the dust before him, and he were not to have everything he wished? Heaps of fellows had been floating round her all the season, but no such large fish as he had risen at the bait; and though she had not particularly distinguished him, still he had only to go in and win the prize. What was it that Gilbert Lloyd had let drop about some rival in the field? O, that man Challoner! Yes, he had himself noticed that there had been a good deal of attention paid in that quarter, and by no means unwillingly received. Queer customer that old Gil! sees everything, by Jove! fancy his spotting that! Good-looking chap, Challoner, and quite enough to say for himself; but, Lord, when it came to the choice between him and the Earl of Ticehurst!

Lord Ticehurst smiled quite pleasantly to himself as this alternative rose in his mind, and flicked his whip in the air over the heads of the roans, causing that spirited pair to plunge in a manner which made the groom (a middle-aged, sober man, with a regard for his neck, and a horror of his master's wild driving) look over the

head of the phaeton in fear and trembling. As
the horses quieted down and settled into their
paces, Lord Ticehurst's spirits sunk simultaneously. Suppose it were all right with the lady,
what about the rest of the people? Not his
following—not Bardolph, Nym, and Pistol, and
the rest of the crew. Lord Ticehurst might not
be a clever man, but he had sufficiently "reckoned up" his *clientèle*, and he knew, whatever
they might think, none of their tongues would
wag. But the outsiders — the "society" people
—what would they say to his bringing a lady
from the boards of the opera to sit at the head
of his table at home, and demand all the respect
due to her rank abroad? They wouldn't like it;
he knew that fast enough. O yes, of course
they'd say that he was not the first who'd done
it, and it had always been a great success
hitherto, and so on; but still he had to look to
his own position and hers, and—by Jove, Lady
Carabas! she'd make it pleasant for them, and
no mistake! Her ladyship liked her *protégée*,
liked to flaunt her in the eyes of rival lion-

hunters, gloried in the success she achieved, and
the excitement she created; but her nephew
knew well enough what her feelings would be if
she had to acknowledge the brilliant *prima donna*
of the opera-house as a relation; if she had to endure the congratulations of her female friends on
the distinguished addition to the family circle
which her kindness and tact had brought about.

What the deuce did it matter to him! The
roans were then pulling well and steadily together, and the phaeton bowled merrily along the
level turnpike-road. What the deuce did it
matter to him! Was not he the Earl of Ticehurst, and was he not to be his own master?
and was not he old enough, and rich enough,
and big swell enough to do what he pleased,
and to take a sight at the world's odd looks,
and pooh-pooh the world's odd remarks? He
was, and he intended to prove it; and after all,
he would like to see one of them to compare with
his pretty Grace. Why, who had they made a
fuss about last season? Alice Farquhar, an
insipid-looking, boiled-veal kind of girl, with her

pale freckled face and her red hair; and Constance Brand, with her big black eyebrows, and her flashing eyes, and her hook-nose — talk about tragedy queens, well, there was Constance Brand cut out for that to a T! Everybody said what a charming thing it was when Alice Farquhar married old Haremarch, and how, ever since, he had been clothed and in his right mind; and as for Constance Brand—well, everyone knew she had saved the family credit by marrying young Klootz, who now called himself Cloote, and who only suffered himself to be reminded by his income that he was lineally descended from old Jacob Klootz, the banker and money-lender of Frankfurt-am-Main. Neither of these girls was to be compared to Miss Lambert, and he was determined that — Lord Ticehurst's spirits sunk again just at this juncture, as the gates of the Hardriggs avenue came within sight.

The Belwethers were very pleasant old-fashioned people, who lived the same life year after year without ever getting tired of it. They

were at Hardriggs, their very pleasant ancestral
seat, from August until the end of March, and
at their very pleasant town-house in Brook-street
from April till the end of July. When in the
country, old Sir Giles shot, fished, and attended
the Quarter-sessions, the Conservative demon-
strations, and the Volunteer reviews of his county.
When in town, he slept a good deal at the
Carlton, and rode a clever cob about the Park
between twelve and two, distinguished for the
bottle-green cutaway coat with velvet-collar, and
the high muslin checked cravat of sixty years
ago. Lady Belwether's character was well
summed up in the phrase "kind old goose,"
which a particular friend applied to her. A
madness for music was the only marked feature
of her disposition: at home she visited all the old
women, and helped the curate, and gave largely
to the Flannel Club, and looked after the schools,
and worried the doctor, and played the har-
monium in the village-church on Sunday; and
in town, what with the opera three nights a-week,
and the Monday Popular Concerts, and the *ma-*

tinées and *soirées musicales* of distinguished creatures, with a dash of Exeter-Hall oratorio, and a *soupçon* of Philharmonic, the old lady's life was one whirl of delight. Lady Belwether had fallen in love with Gertrude at first sight. She was by no means a gushing old lady, nor, though so devoted to music, had she ever made the acquaintance of any professional. Hitherto she had always stood on her dignity when such a proposition had been made to her. She had no doubt, she used to say, that the artists in question were pleasant people in their way, but that was not her way. However, the first glance at Miss Lambert made the old lady wild to know her: there never was such a sweet face—so interesting, so classical—yes, the old lady might say, so holy; "and her voice, my dear, it gives me the notion of an angel singing." So, worthy old Lady Belwether having ascertained that Miss Lambert was perfectly "correct" and ladylike, procured an introduction to her, and commenced heaping upon her a series of kindnesses which culminated in the invitation to Hardriggs. This invitation was accepted principally by the advice of Lord Sandilands, who had known the Belwethers all his life, and who felt that Gertrude could not enjoy the quiet and fresh air requisite after her London season with more thoroughly respectable people.

It was after the invitation had been given and accepted that Lady Belwether began to feel a little nervous and uncomfortable about what she had done. For in the pride of her heart and the warmth of her admiration for Gertrude, she told everybody that dear Miss Lambert was coming to them at Hardriggs in the autumn. Among others, she mentioned the fact to Miss Belwether, Sir Giles's sister, a dreadful old woman who lived in a boarding-house at Brighton, in order to be in the closest proximity to her "pastor," the Reverend Mr. Tophet, and who uttered a yelp of horror at the announcement. "I have said nothing, Maria," said this horrible old person, "to your gaddings-about and the frivolous style of your existence, but I must lift up my voice when you tell me you are about to receive a stage-player as your guest." "Stage-player" is an awkward word to be thrown at the head of a leader of county society, and it hit home, and rather staggered dear old Lady Bel-wether; not that the gallant old lady for an instant entertained the notion of giving up her intended guest, or suffered herself to appear the least abashed in the eyes of her antagonist. "It's a mere matter of taste, my dear Martha," she replied; "for my own part, I would sooner as-sociate with a lady who, though a singer, is undoubtedly a lady, than with a man who calls himself a minister, who was a shoemaker, and who always must be a vulgar boor." Having fired which raking shot at the Reverend Tophet, the old lady sailed away and closed the conver-sation.

But she felt that it would be a great advan-tage if she could have someone staying in the house at the same time with Miss Lambert, whose presence would prove an effectual check on the ridiculous gossip likely to be prevalent in the county. The lay element would be excellently represented in the respectably dull and decorous people who were coming; but there was wanting an infusion of the clerical element, which could best be met by inviting Sir Giles's old friend the Dean of Burwash. Henry Asprey, Dean of Burwash, had been known as "Felix" Asprey at school and college, from his uninterrupted run of luck. The son of a poor solicitor, a good-looking idle lad, of capital manners and address, but with very little real talent, he had won an exhibition from his school, a scholarship, a fellowship, and a double-second at the University, no one knew how. He had taken orders, and travelled as tutor to the then Premier's son through Egypt and the Holy Land; on his return had published a little book of very weak poems, under the title *Palm-leaves and Dates*, which, with his usual luck, happened to hit the very bad taste of the day, and went through several editions. His friend the Premier gave him a good living, and he had scarcely been inducted into it when he won the heart of a very rich widow, whom he married, and whom, with his usual luck, within the course of four years he buried, inheriting her fortune of three thousand a-year. It was to console him in his deep affliction that his friend the Premier, just then quitting office for the third and last time, bestowed upon him the Deanery of Burwash. He was now some fifty years old, tall, thin, and eminently aristocratic-looking; had a long transparent hand, which was generally clasping his chin, and a soft persuasive voice. He liked music and poetry, and good dinners; was found at private views of picture-exhibitions; belonged to the Athenæum Club; and liked to be seen there conversing with professional literary men. People said he would be a Bishop some day, and he thought so himself—he did not see why not; he would have looked well in his robes, spoken well in the House of Lords, and never committed himself by the utterance of any extreme opinion. That was a thing he had avoided all his life, and to it much of the secret of his success might be ascribed. His sermons were eloquent—his friends said " sound," his enemies " empty;" he deplored the division in the Church with sympathetic face and elegant gesture; but he never gave adhesion to either side, and showed more skill in parrying home-questions than in any other action of his life.

Such was Dean Asprey, to whom Lady Belwether wrote an invitation to Hardriggs, telling him frankly that Miss Grace Lambert would be one of the guests, and asking if he had any objection to meet her. The Dean's reply, written in the neatest hand on the thickest cream-laid notepaper, arrived by return of post. He accepted the invitation as heartily as it was given ("Genial creature!" said dear old Lady Belwether); he fully appreciated dear Lady Belwether's frankness about her guest, for he was aware—how could he fail to be?—of the censoriousness of the world towards persons of his calling. He had, however, made it his rule through life, and he intended to pursue the same course until the end, to shape his conduct according to the dictates of that still small voice of his conscience rather than at the bidding of the

world. ("The dear!" said Lady Belwether.)
He should therefore have the greatest pleasure
in making the acquaintance of Miss Grace
Lambert, of whom he had already heard the
most favourable accounts, not merely as regarded
her great genius, but her exemplary conduct.
And he was, with kindest regards to Giles, his
dear Lady Belwether's most sincere friend, Henry
Asprey. "A Christian gentleman," said the old
lady, with tears of delight standing in her eyes
as she finished the letter; "and Martha to talk
of her stage-players and Tophets indeed, when a
man like that does not mind!"

The Belwethers were rather astonished when,
just after the party had sat down to luncheon,
they heard Lord Ticehurst announced. For
though there was a certain similarity of sporting
tastes between him and Sir Giles, the disparity
of age caused them to move in widely different
sets; while Lady Belwether knew his lordship as
the nephew and one of the principal attendants
on, and abettors of, Lady Carabas, whom the old
lady held in great aversion. "One of the new

style of ladies, my dear," she used to say with a sniff of disdain; "finds women's society too dull for her, must live amongst men, talks slang, and I daresay smokes, if one only knew." However, they both received the young nobleman with considerable *empressement;* and Lord Ticehurst, on taking his seat at the luncheon-table, found that he knew most of the assembled party. The Dean was almost the only one with whom he had not a previous acquaintance; and Lord Ticehurst had scarcely whispered to Lady Belwether a request to know who was the clerical party on his left, when the Dean turned round and introduced himself as an old friend of the late Lord Ticehurst's. "I used to meet your father at Lady Walsingham's receptions when Lord Walsingham was Premier, and he allowed me to call him my very good friend. We had certain tastes in common which bound us together—geology and mineralogy, for instance. You are not a geologist, I believe, my lord?"

"Well, no," said Lord Ticehurst frankly; "that ain't my line."

"N-no," said the Dean. "Well, we all have our different tastes—*tot homines, quot sententiæ.* Your father was a man who was passionately fond of science; indeed, I often used to wonder how a man absorbed as he was in what generally proves to others the all-engrossing study of politics could find time for the discussion of scientific propositions, and for the attendance at the lectures of the Royal Institution. But your father was a man of no ordinary calibre; he was—"

"O yes, he was a great gun at science and electricity, and all that kind of thing, at least so I've been told. Excuse me for half a minute; I want to get some of that ham I see on the sideboard." And Lord Ticehurst rose from the seat, to which he did not return after he had helped himself, preferring a vacant place at the other end of the table, by the side of Sir Giles Belwether, whose conversation about hunting and racing proved far more entertaining to his lordship. Moreover, from his new position he could keep a better view of Miss Lambert, who did not, he was pleased to observe, seem particularly gratified or amused at the rapid fire of conversation kept up by the young men on either side of her.

When luncheon was over, and the party rose and dispersed, Lord Ticehurst was seized upon by Sir Giles, who took him to the stables, expatiating lengthily and wearily on the merits of his cattle; and it was not until late in the afternoon that the visitor could make his escape from his host. He thought that he would have had his journey for nothing, seeing no chance of getting a private interview with Miss Lambert, when on his return to the house to see if he could find Lady Belwether, to whom he intended making his adieux, he heard the sound of a piano, and recognised the prelude of a favourite ballad of Gertrude's. Before the song could begin, Lord Ticehurst had entered the room, and found Miss Lambert, as he expected, alone at the piano. Gertrude looked round at the opening of the door, and when she saw who it was, half rose from her seat.

"Pray don't move, Miss Lambert," said Lord

Ticehurst, approaching her; "pray don't let me disturb you."

"You don't disturb me in the least, Lord Ticehurst," said Gertrude, sitting down again. "I was merely amusing myself. I had not even the business excuse of being 'at practice.'"

"Don't let me interfere, then. Amuse yourself and me at the same time. Do now, it will be a charity; 'pon my word it will."

"No, no, no; I'm not so cruel as that. I know the terrible infliction music is to you in London. I've watched too often the martyr-like manner in which you've suffered under long classical pieces, and the self-denying way in which you have applauded at the end of them, without deliberately exposing you to more torture in the country."

"Assure you you're wrong, Miss Lambert; but I'm too happy to think you've done me the honour to watch me at all, to go into the question. No, please don't go. If you won't sing to me, may I speak to you?"

Gertrude, who had again half-risen, turned

round to him with a look of wonder in her eyes.
"May you speak to me, Lord Ticehurst? Why,
of course!"

The answer was so manifestly simple and
genuine, that it quite took Lord Ticehurst aback,
and there was a moment's pause before he said,
"Thanks, yes—you're very good. I wanted to
speak to you—wanted to say something rather
particular to you, in point of fact."

The hesitation in his manner, an odd conscious
look in his face, had revealed the object of his
visit. Gertrude knew what he was about to say,
but she remained perfectly calm and unembar-
rassed, merely saying,

"Pray speak, Lord Ticehurst; I am quite at
your service."

"Thanks very much—kind of you to say so,
I'm sure. Fact of the matter is, Miss Lambert,
ever since I've had the pleasure of knowing you
I've been completely stumped, don't you know?—
bowled over, and that kind of thing. I suppose
you've noticed it; fellows at the club chaff most
awfully, you know, and I can't stand it any longer;

and, in short, I've come to ask you if—if you'll marry me, and that kind of thing."

"You do me great honour, Lord Ticehurst," commenced Gertrude; "very great honour—"

"O," interrupted his lordship, "don't you think about that; that's what they said at White's, but I said that was all d—d stuff—I beg your pardon, Miss Lambert; all nonsense I mean—about honour, and all that. Why," he went on to say, having worked himself up into a state of excitement, "of course I know I'm an earl, and that kind of thing. I can't help knowing about my—my station in life, and you'd think me a great ass if I pretended I didn't; but when you're my wife, you'll be—I mean to say you'll grace it and adorn it—and—and there's not one in the whole list fit to be named along with you, or to hold a candle to you."

"I cannot thank you sufficiently for this expression of kind feeling towards me, Lord Ticehurst," said Gertrude. "No, hear me for one minute;" as he endeavoured again to interrupt her. "Ever since you have known me you have treated me with the utmost courtesy and kindness, and you have now done me the greatest possible honour. You may judge, then, how painful it is to me—" Lord Ticehurst's jaw and hat here dropped simultaneously—"how painful it is to me to be compelled to decline that honour."

"To—to decline it?"

"To decline it."

"To say no!"

"To say no."

"Then you refuse me! Case of chalks, by Jove! Miss Lambert, I—I'm sorry I've troubled you," said Lord Ticehurst, picking up his hat and making for the door. "I hope you won't think anything of it, I—good-morning!—Damme if I know whether I'm on my head or my heels," he added when he got outside, and was alone.

Lord Ticehurst was so completely *bouleversé* that he scarcely knew how he got to his phaeton, or how he tooled the roans, who were additionally frisky after the Belwether oats, down the avenue. He knew nothing until he got to the gate, on the other side of which was an open fly. He looked vacantly at its occupants, but started as he recognised Lord Sandilands and Miles Challoner.

"O, that's it, is it?" said his lordship to himself. "Damme, old Gil was right again!"

CHAPTER IX.

DIEU DISPOSE.

THE effect of Miles Challoner's startling communication upon Lord Sandilands was very great; but the long-cultivated habit of self-command enabled him to conceal its extent and somewhat of its nature from his younger friend. It was fortunate that Miles was just then so much engrossed with his love, so full of the hope of the success of his suit, so relieved and encouraged by discovering that Lord Sandilands did not attempt to dissuade him from a project in which he had felt very doubtful whether he should have the support of a man of the world—and though nothing would have induced him to abandon that project, Lord Sandilands' acquiescence made a wonderful difference to him in the present, and would, he felt, be of weighty importance in the

future,—that he was not keenly observant of the
old nobleman. As soon as it was possible, Lord
Sandilands got rid of Miles, but not until he had
received from the young man a grateful acknowledgment of his kindness, and until they had
finally agreed on the expedition to Hardriggs for
the following day.

When he was quite alone, the familiar friend
of Miles Challoner's father gave way to the
feelings with which this revelation had filled him.
This, then, was the explanation of the instinctive
aversion he had felt towards Gilbert Lloyd—fate
had brought him in contact with the man whose
story he alone of living men knew, and under
circumstances which might have terrible import.
The one hope of his dead friend—that the brothers
might never meet—had been defeated; the fear
which had troubled him in his later days had been
fulfilled. If Miles Challoner's impression concerning this man should be correct—if indeed he was
or intended to become a suitor to Gertrude, a
fresh complication of an extremely dangerous
nature—knowing what he knew, he could well

appreciate that danger might arise. The skeleton was wearing flesh again, and stalking very close by the old man now. Hitherto only the strong sympathy which had united him with Miles Challoner and his father—his friendship for the latter had been one of the strongest and deepest feelings of a life which had, on the whole, been superficial —made the fate of the outcast son and brother a subject of any interest to Lord Sandilands. He might have turned up at any time, and this unfortunate meeting and recognition between the brothers have taken place, and beyond the unpleasantness of the occurrence, and the necessity he should have recognised for impressing upon Miles as stringently as possible the importance of observing his father's prohibition, he would not have felt himself personally concerned. But Gertrude! the girl whom he had come to love with such true fatherly feeling and solicitude—the girl who had brought into his superficial life such mingled feelings of pain and pleasure—what if she were about to be involved in this family mystery and misery? Very seldom in the course of

his existence had Lord Sandilands experienced
such acute pain, such a sensation of helpless terror, as this supposition inspired. Supposing that
Miles Challoner was right in the dread which
Gilbert Lloyd's manner with regard to Gertrude
had awakened in him,—and the eyes of a lover
not sure of his own position, and anxiously on the
look-out for possible rivals, were likely to be more
acute and more accurate than those of an old gentleman much out of practice in the subtleties of
the tender passion, and without the spur to his
perceptions of suspicion,—supposing he was really
in love with Gertrude, and that by any horrible
chance Gertrude should prefer him to Miles!
Very unpleasant physical symptoms of disturbance
manifested themselves after Lord Sandilands had
fully taken this terrible hypothesis into consideration, and for a time the old gentleman felt that
whether it was gout or apoplexy which was about
to claim him for its own was a mere question of
detail. He had lived so long without requiring to
test the strength of his nerves, without having any
very strong or urgent demand made upon him for

the exercise of his feelings, that anything of the
kind now decidedly disagreed with him, and he
went to bed in a rueful state of mind, and a shaky
condition of body. The night brought him calm-
ness and counsel, and the symptoms of illness
passed off sufficiently for him to resolve on keeping the engagement he had made with Miles for
the following day. "The sooner his mind is at
ease, the sooner will mine be, on his account and
my own." Thus ran Lord Sandilands' thoughts
as he lay awake, listening against his will to the
splash of the sea, and inclined to blame its mono-
tonous murmur for the nervousness which had
him in its grip. "I suppose it's not the right
thing for me to help Miles to marry Gertrude—
my old friend would not have liked the notion of
his son and heir's marrying my natural daughter;
but what can I do? The young fellow is not
like other men of his age and position; in fact,
he isn't, strictly speaking, I suppose, a 'young'
fellow at all. If he were, and resembled the
young men of the day a little more, I fancy he
never would have thought of marrying her. And

then there's an awful blot upon the Challoners, too—and she is such a charming girl, no tongue has ever dared to wag against her. Suppose I did not encourage it, that I set myself against it, what could I do? I have literally no right in Miles's case, and none that I can acknowledge in Gertrude's, and I should only make them both dislike me, without preventing the marriage in the least. I wish—because of what poor old Mark would have thought—that they had never met; but I can't go beyond that—no, I can't. But if she cares for that wretch, good heavens! what shall I do?" The old man put his shrunken hands up to his bald temples, and twisted his head about on his pillow, and groaned in his solitude and perplexity. "Must I threaten him with exposure, and so drive him out of the country? or must I tell her the truth about herself, and ask her to believe, on the faith of my unexplained assertion, that the man is one whom she must never think of marrying?"

The position was one of indisputable difficulty the "pleasant vice"—that long-ago story of a dead woman, deceived indeed, but with no extraordinary cruelty, a story which had not troubled Lord Sandilands' conscience very much — had manufactured itself finally into a whip of stout dimensions and stinging quality, and he was getting a very sufficient taste of it just now.

Miles must try his luck. That was the only conclusion which could be immediately reached. If he could sleep a little, he might feel all right in the morning, and be able to accompany him to Hardriggs. If he were not well enough, Miles must go all the same. If the young man should feel surprise and curiosity at finding his old friend so impatient, it could not be helped; it must pass as a vagary of an old man's. But Miles would not remark anything; the vagary was sufficiently cognate to his own humour and his own purposes to pass unnoticed.

When Lord Sandilands and Miles Challoner arrived at Hardriggs on the following day, a close observer would have discerned that they were both under a strong impression of some kind.

Lord Sandilands was not feeling well by any means, but he had assured Miles the drive would do him good, and he had found his indisposition so far useful, that it explained and excused his being very silent on the way. Neither was Miles much inclined to talk. He was of an earnest nature, never at any time voluble, and when under the influence of strong feeling silence was congenial to him. He well understood that the revelation he had made to Lord Sandilands on the preceding day had produced a startling and disagreeable effect; and having perceived plainly, beyond the possibility of doubt, that the secret which he so earnestly desired to know was in Lord Sandilands' possession, and was of a darker and direr nature than he had ever guessed at, but was, at the same time, quite as securely beyond his reach as ever, he made up his mind to let the subject drop. Unless this man had cut him out, or was likely to cut him out with Grace Lambert, he had no power to harm him. The truth was, Miles Challoner was very sincerely and heartily in love, and he had as little power as in-

clination to occupy his thoughts for long at a time
with anyone but Grace, with any speculation but
his chance of success with her. Luckily, Sir Giles
and Lady Belwether were the least observant of
human beings. Sir Giles was stupid to an extent
which is not to be realised except by those who
understand the bucolic gentry of our favoured
land, and Lady Belwether was—though superior,
as we have seen, to her baronet in intelligence,
and distinguished by a taste for music—very short-
sighted. Close observers were therefore not "on
hand," when Lord Sandilands and Miles arrived
at Hardriggs. Sir Giles was contemplating the
turnips at a distant point of his "pretty little
place;" Miss Lambert had gone out into the
garden, or the lime-walk, the servants said, some
time before; and Lady Belwether and Mrs. Bloxam
were in the morning-room.

Lord Sandilands did not lose much time in
arranging the situation as he wished it to be
arranged, so far as Miles was concerned—his
consummate ease of manner, which Miles admired to the point of envy, rendered any little

disposition of affairs of that kind a very simple proceeding to him. Miles was despatched in search of Sir Giles, Mrs. Bloxam was begged on no account to interfere with Miss Lambert's saunter in the garden—they might join her presently, perhaps—and Lady Belwether was engaged in a discussion upon the comparative merits of "our" native composers, within a space of time whose brevity would have been surprising to anyone unacquainted with the rapid action of a fixed purpose combined with good manners. Mrs. Bloxam had directed one searching glance at Lord Sandilands on his entrance, and, as she withdrew her eyes, she said to herself, "Something has happened. He wants to speak to me; but I had rather he did not, so he sha'n't." And strange to say, though he made a protracted visit to Hardriggs that day, Lord Sandilands did not succeed in getting an opportunity of speaking a word to Mrs. Bloxam. This annoyed him a good deal. "Confound the woman!" he said to himself; "either Mrs. Bloxam is too stupid to see that I want to speak to her, or Lady Belwether is too clever to leave off talking!" In his capacity of gooseberry-picker, Lord Sandilands was led on this occasion into anything but pleasant pastures.

The shortest way to the turnips, just then occupying the mind and demanding the presence of Sir Giles Belwether, fortunately lay through the garden, otherwise Miles Challoner might not have profited so readily and unsuspected by the strategy of his clever old friend. Through a side-gate of the garden the lime-walk was to be gained, and as Miles closed that gate behind him he caught sight of Grace Lambert. She was walking slowly along in the shadow of the trees, her head bent down in a thoughtful attitude. Miles went quickly towards her, and she looked up and recognised him with a slight start and a vivid blush; in fact, with the kind of recognition which takes place when the person who intrudes upon a reverie happens to be its subject. Gertrude had been thinking of Miles—she thought of him very often now; and the interview which had taken place between herself and Lord Ticehurst had made her think of him more seriously than ever. She loved him.

She did not deny the truth, or palter with it, or fail to recognise its consequences. She had mistaken pleased and excited fancy and flattered vanity for love once, but this was nothing of the kind. She knew this was true love, because she thought of *him*, not of herself; because she did not hope, but feared he loved her. How would she have listened to such an avowal from Miles's lips as that which, made by Lord Ticehurst, had produced mere contempt, and a desire to get rid of it and him as quickly as possible? Gertrude had accepted her position in such perfect good faith, that its difficulties never presented themselves in a practical form at all; and she pondered this matter now in her heart, as if she were really the free unmarried girl she seemed to the world. If he should come to her and tell her a love-tale, what should she say to him? She had asked herself the question many times and had not found the answer, when, raising her eyes at the sound of steps, she met those of Miles Challoner, and saw in them what he had come to say.

There was manifest embarrassment on both

sides, and each was distinctly conscious of its cause. Why could they not meet to-day as they had met so often before? Why were the ordinary commonplaces so hard to think of and so incoherently said? Gertrude was the first to recover her composure. She asked Miles if Lord Sandilands had come with him; and on his saying he had, and was then in the house, she turned in that direction, and said something about going in to see him. But Miles checked her steps by standing still.

"Don't go into the house," he said; "he does not expect you. Let us walk this way; let me speak to you." She glanced at him, and silently complied. She knew it all now, and she began to feel what it was that she must say, and what it would cost her to say it. She felt his eyes upon her, and the delicate colour faded away from her face.

Neither she nor Miles Challoner could have told afterwards, or even exactly recalled in their thoughts, the words then spoken between them. He told her how he had loved her from the first —he who had never loved before—and how fear and hope had alternated in his heart until now, when hope was the stronger, and he had determined to tell her how all his happiness, all his life, was in her hands. He spoke with the frank manliness of his nature, and Gertrude's heart thrilled as she listened to him with intense pain, with keen delight. At least he loved her well and worthily; nothing could deprive her of that exquisite knowledge. She would, she must, put away the wine of life offered to her parched lips, but she knew its sweetness, had seen the splendour and the sparkle of it.

A thousand thoughts, innumerable emotions, crowded upon her, as she listened to the words of Miles; but when he prayed her to speak and let him know his fate, prayed her with eagerness and passion, but with hope that was almost confidence, then she put them all down with her strong will, and addressed herself to her task. She drew the hand which he had taken away from his hold, and told him in one short sentence that she could not give him the answer he desired.

"You cannot, Grace? You refuse me!" he said hoarsely. "You tell me, then, that I have deceived myself?"

"No," she said, "I do not. Let us sit here awhile"—she seated herself on a bench under a lime-tree as she spoke — "and let me speak frankly and freely to you, as you deserve."

Miles obeyed her with bewilderment. What was she going to say? She would not marry him, and yet he had *not* deceived himself! She was deadly pale, and he might have heard the beating of her heart; but she was quite firm, and she turned her steady eyes upon him un-falteringly.

"There is only one thing you can say to me," he said, "if you persevere in forbidding me to hope —that is, to send me out of your sight for ever."

"Perhaps," was her reply; "but listen. I have said you don't deceive yourself, and I mean it. I know you love me; I know what perfect sincerity there is in you—hush! let me speak— and I—I do love you—you have not mistaken me, I have not misled you."

"Then what does anything else matter?" said Miles, and he caught her hands and kissed them unresisted, unrebuked. "With that assurance, Grace, surely you will not refuse me?"

"I must," she answered. "Have patience with me; I will tell you why. It is for your own sake."

"My own sake!" he exclaimed passionately; "you deprive me of all hope and happiness for my own sake! I shall need patience indeed to understand that."

"It is true, nevertheless. I could not marry you, Miles Challoner, without doing you a great injury; and I love you too well, much more and better than myself, to do that. Take that assurance, and believe that nothing can shake my determination. My fate is decided, my way of life is quite fixed. I shall never be your wife, never, never, never!"—his face was hidden in his hands, he did not see the suffering which broke all control and showed itself plainly in her every feature—"but I shall never love you less, or anyone but you." The low distinct tones of her voice thrilled him with a horrid sense of hopelessness. She spoke as one who had taken an irrevocable resolution.

"What do you · mean?" he said. "You must tell me more than this. What do you mean by doing me an injury? I protest I have not the faintest notion of your meaning. It cannot be—" He hesitated, and she took up his words.

"Because you are a gentleman of old name and a responsible position in society, and I am a singer, an actress, a woman with no name and no station, you would say. Yes, it is precisely for this cause, which you think impossible. I know you don't regard any of these things, but the world does; and the man I love shall never be censured by the world for me."

How well it was, she thought, how fortunate, that such a real genuine difficulty did exist; that she could give some explanation which he might be induced to receive.

"Then you would make me wretched for the sake of the world, even if what you say of my

position and your own were true? And it is not.
Is your genius nothing? Is your fame nothing?
I speak now as reasonably as yourself; not as a
man who holds you peerless, far removed above
all the world, but as one discussing a question
open to argument. What am I in comparison
to the men who would be proud to offer you
rank and wealth? What have I to give you
that others could not give a thousandfold?"

"You give me all I value, all I care for,"
she said; "but I must not take it. You must
not, you shall not, deceive yourself. My genius,
as you call it, my fame, are real things in their
way and in their sphere, but they are not of any
account in yours. Ask your friend Lord Sandilands; he is a kind friend to me also, and a man
who knows the world thoroughly; and he will
tell you I am right."

"No, he won't!" said Miles triumphantly.
"No, he won't! He will tell *you*, on the contrary, that *you* are quite wrong; he will tell you
that he knows I love you, and have dared to
hope, to believe that you love me. He will tell

you that I have told him what is my dearest
hope, and that he shares it; and more, Grace,
more than that, he will tell you that he came
here with me to-day on purpose that I might
learn my fate, and be no longer in suspense;
and that he is on duty at this moment, keeping
the old ladies in talk, just to give me this
precious opportunity. Now, where are all your
arguments? where are my wise friends? where
is this terrible world to whom we are to be
sacrificed? You have nothing more to say,
Grace; your 'never, never, never!' cannot hurt
me any more."

For one brief moment he triumphed. For
one moment his arm was around her, and his
lips were pressed to hers. But the next she had
started from his embrace, and stood pale and
breathless before him.

"Is this really true?" she said; "does Lord
Sandilands approve?" She asked him only to
gain a moment's time for thought; she was
terribly disconcerted by this complication, it
increased her difficulties immensely. But Miles

saw in the question only a symptom of yielding, only a proof of his victory.

"Yes, yes," he said eagerly, "it is true; it is indeed! He is the only real friend I have in the world, the only man whose opinion I care for, and he is on my side. Now, Grace, you must yield; you cannot refuse me."

She stood for a moment motionless and silent. Then her nerves, generally so strong, so completely under control, gave way. The violence of the struggle, the intensity of the pain she was suffering, that overwhelming remembrance of the past, the agonising sense of what might have been, but was now quite impossible, the feebleness of the only weapon which she could venture to use in this battle in which her own heart was her adversary,—all these overcame her, and she sunk upon the bench in a helpless agony of tears.

Terrified by her distress, Miles Challoner knelt before her, and implored her to explain the cause of this sudden grief. But all his prayers were vain. She wept convulsively for many minutes, and was literally unable to speak. When at last she conquered the passion of tears, she felt and looked so very ill that he became alarmed on a fresh score.

"You are ill," he said; "shall I go for Mrs. Bloxam? Shall I take you to the house?"

She made a sign with her hand that he should not speak, then leaned her head against the bench, and closed her eyes. He stood by, awkward and silent, watching her. After a little while she sat up, and said faintly:

"Will you leave me? Go away from me for the present—I am ill; but it is only from agitation. Let me be alone for a while; you shall see me again when I am able."

"Of course I will leave you, if you wish it," said Miles, with all the timidity and embarrassment of a man in the presence of feminine weakness and suffering; "but I am afraid you are not fit to be left alone."

"I am indeed," she urged, and her face grew whiter as she spoke; "I shall recover myself, if I am left alone. Don't fear for me. Go to the

house, and do not say you have seen me. Go
by the lime-walk into the avenue; I will go by
the garden. No one will see me; and if I can
get to my room and lie down for a little, I shall
be quite well. Pray, pray go."

She put her hands before her face, and Miles
saw a quick shudder pass over her from head
to foot. He was afraid to go, afraid to stay; at
length he obeyed her, and took the way towards
the house which she had indicated, feeling be-
wildered and alarmed.

When Miles Challoner reëntered the drawing-
room at Hardriggs he found Lord Sandilands still
there, held in durance by Lady Belwether and
Mrs. Bloxam. Lord Sandilands had found his
hostess immovable, and no other afternoon callers
had had the kindness to come and partially re-
lease him. Mrs. Bloxam kept her eyes and her
fingers steadily and unremittingly engaged with
her fancy-work, and Lady Belwether persisted in
discoursing on music and religion. With his
accustomed philosophy Lord Sandilands accepted
the situation, consoling himself by the reflection

that a day or two could not make any difference in what he had to say to Mrs. Bloxam, and that the chief object of his present exertions had at least been secured, for he entertained a satisfactory conviction that Miles and Gertrude had met "somewhere about." Miles returned too soon, in one sense, for the old gentleman's wishes; he would rather have found him utterly oblivious of time; in that case, and if no consideration of anybody's convenience had occurred to Miles, Lord Sandilands would have felt confidence in the prospering of the suit. But Miles came in looking as little like a successful and happy lover as he could look, and Lord Sandilands perceived in an instant that things had gone wrong. He did not give Miles time to speak before he rose, and saying, " You have clear ideas of time, Miles; we ought to be back before now.—Business, Lady Belwether, business — you don't understand its claims, happily for you.—Good-bye, Mrs. Bloxam; tell Miss Lambert I am sorry not to have seen her;" he got himself and his melancholy, and indeed frightened-looking, companion out of the room and out of the house.

"Now tell me all about it," said Lord Sandilands to Miles when they were in the carriage; "what has happened? You have seen her, of course?"

"Yes," said Miles ruefully, and then with much embarrassment he told Lord Sandilands what had occurred.

The narrative perplexed and distressed the listener. He understood Gertrude's feelings up to a certain point, but no farther; he could not understand why Miles's representations of his advocacy of his suit had had no effect in moderating her apprehensions of the world's view of such a marriage. He could say little or nothing to console Miles, but he told him he did not regard Miss Lambert's decision as final, or the nervous attack which had so alarmed him as of any import.

"I will see her, and have it out with her," said Lord Sandilands to himself; "and if it is necessary for her happiness's sake and that of Miles, I will tell her the truth."

Robson and Son, Printers, Pancras Road, N.W.